Waypoints

ADAM OUSTON is a writer of fiction and non-fiction, and the recipient of the 2014 Erica Bell Literary Award as well as the manuscript prize at the Tasmanian Premier's Literary Awards in 2017. He holds a PhD and has worked as a copywriter, editor and bookseller. As a musician he performs as Costume. He lives in Hobart, Tasmania.

First published in Great Britain in 2022 by Splice,
54 George Street, Innerleithen EH44 6LJ.

The right of Adam Ouston to be identified as the author of
this work has been asserted in accordance with
Section 77 of the Copyright, Designs and Patents Act 1988.

Paperback Edition: ISBN 978-1-9196398-4-0
Ebook Edition: ISBN 978-1-9196398-5-7

Waypoints

Adam Ouston

SPLICE

For Emily

These new dimensions are Up.

— FM-2030

Up, up the long, delirious burning blue...

— John Gillespie Magee, Jr.

IT'S BIZARRE BECAUSE NOW, in our age of information, when any fact, datum or titbit is literally at our fingertips, and the price for being deemed wrong grows mightier by the day; when any idle curiosity or bagatelle can be satisfied in an instant, invariably leading to further idle curiosities and bagatelles, taking you deeper into the goldmine of a seemingly limitless supply; when it's more or less understandable that, for most of us, there really is no excuse for not knowing anything, it's all there, all you have to do is look it up; now, in an age when the sweep of history is laid out before us, notwithstanding all the caveats, hesitations and conflicting perspectives, of those who know about the airborne exploits of the Great Harry Houdini—illusionist, self-promoter, dispeller of frauds and inveterate daredevil—more people seem to know that the Master of Mystery *didn't* actually get the record for the first controlled flight of a powered aircraft in Australia than know who in fact *did*. The suggestion that the Handcuff King had been beaten to the punch came as a surprise to me, but the more I looked into the matter, the more I found that the record held by the cunning escapologist had become disputed, qualified and sometimes even dismissed outright, given all the fuss over aviation at the dawn of human flight, records being attempted and broken, new heights being reached, both literally and metaphorically—really, the world at the time was so taken by all things aircraft-related that many newspapers had sections headed 'Flight' to discuss global air events; who went up where and in what, which awards were on offer and with what prize money—indeed, there was so much wonder surrounding aviation, and people were so awestruck at seeing their fellow humans take to the skies, and the hype was so intense, that it is

1

conceivable that official records do not quite match the events as they really transpired; which is why there is some conjecture from certain quarters surrounding Houdini's attempt to soar over Australian soil, the curious upshot being that while it might be common knowledge that the great mystifier held the record (or holds it still, depending on who you ask) the very fact that it is disputed seems to be the fact worth knowing, maybe because it implies greater familiarity with the subject, which in turn suggests that the more valuable fact regarding Houdini's flight on 18 March 1910 at Diggers Rest in Victoria, just north of Melbourne, coincidentally near the present-day Tullamarine Airport, isn't what something *is* but rather what something *isn't*. "That's the spot," people say, "that's the very paddock where Harry Houdini—born Erik Weisz, of course, in Hungary in 1874, one of seven children, the youngest of whom, Carrie, was left almost completely blind following a childhood accident, though both the accident and whatever came of her (some say she lived her life as a ghostwriter) is an even deeper mystery than the aura surrounding her elder brother with the mesmerising eyes— that's the precise location, look it up, that's where Harry Houdini, born Erik Weisz in landlocked Hungary in 1874 only to travel to America four years later, with his family, including Carrie, and who, five years after that, at the age of nine, giving his first public performance as a trapeze artist, crowned himself 'The Prince of the Air'—how fitting that moniker would become some twenty-seven years down the track when he arrived at Diggers Rest, north of Melbourne, near today's Tullamarine, where if you go up there now you can pinpoint the selfsame paddock in which Harry Houdini (there's a memorial; two, actually), who also went by Erik Weisz, Ehrich Weiss and Harry Weiss, not to mention Prince of the Air— why not King of the Air we'll never know—if you hop on a train or a bus or rent a car, you can zero in on the coordinates where the Great Houdini—all the way from Europe via America via Europe where, incidentally, he picked up the French-made aircraft, a Voisin biplane, which he'd flown in Hamburg before sailing off, plane in cargo, for the Great Southern Land aboard the P&O liner SS *Malwa*, his wife Bess was by now drinking heavily and out of reach, while at thirty-six the great mystifier and *de*mystifier (he maintained it was all just trickery and sleight of hand, not magic at all) was starting to feel that vaudeville had had its day, and that maybe he himself, the Great H.H., had also had his day, with perpetually sore wrists from escaping handcuffs, aching shoulders from daily dis-locations, a ruined lower back that would only get worse as the years went by, and a tender derrière from having an infected boil lanced barely a month prior; which is to say that as he stood on the blustery deck, hands in pockets, gazing out over the endless silver sea—with Bess sleeping it off in their cabin—his mind was turning more and more to thoughts of death: his own, yes, but also the death of vaudeville, the extinction of a craft he'd spent his life honing, the silencing of the crowds, and the end of wonders—which was strange in itself because he would have been the first to admit that death had been, from the very beginning, his constant companion, one he'd actively courted and flirted with, for it was the threat of his imminent demise that kept derrières on seats—but now aboard the *Malwa*, the wind making his receding hair seem possessed, he was contemplating the end of all that, the death of death, the threat of choking, drowning, suffocating suddenly humdrum, faced with the dark maws of a yawning audience, he might have even considered flinging himself seaward if it were not for these fantastic new flying machines that promised to give a lift to his stalling career, his stalling life. Germany had been a practice run, and while he skimmed beneath those monochrome Teutonic skies, he imagined himself soaring over the sun-soaked paddock and disinterested live-stock half-an-hour north of Melbourne, picturing the khaki scrub blurred by speed and the black dots of skyward-gazing spectators,

the throng of enthusiasts cheering him on—he could hear them
cheering, just like they'd done in theatres from Boston to Belfast—
the men waving their bowler hats up at him or else at God, who
could tell the difference?—why not God of the Air we'll never
know—because that's what it would have felt like being up there,
a god, a pioneer!, when the rest of the world had been discovered,
when every continent, country and capital city had been canvassed
and coined, when there was practically not a blade of grass that
had not bent under an explorer's boot, here he was, the Great Harry
Houdini, Prince of the Air, up among clouds, the final frontier, another death-defying feat (you always had to stay one ahead of your
rivals), a new and untapped way to die, a sudden shot in the arm
for the listless Handcuff King and his expectant audience; surely he
must have felt like a god among children with the power of lightning in his veins, he could imagine it up above Hamburg, could see
it on the insides of his eyelids, and you can too, if you go there to
the veritable, the *verifiable*, dot on the map, north of Melbourne, that
waypoint of waypoints, and *look up* and exclaim that right there,
that's the very spot where Houdini—though he often went by other
names; I prefer Erik Weisz with that particular and peculiar and
very Hungarian 'z,' as did his beloved mother Cecília—where, at
last, Houdini did *not* become the first man to conduct a controlled
flight over Australian soil." It's bizarre because, in this day and age,
in which everything is available to us, every fact, datum and tidbit,
and there's no excuse for not knowing anything, it's all there for
you, you don't even have to spell it correctly, in fact you don't have
to spell it at all, you can just mutter a question into the æther and
the æther itself will answer, which is perhaps the greatest trick in
the history of magic, speak to the air and the air speaks back—ask
not now who are the Gods of the Air!—shout into the darkness and
the darkness shouts back, because that's all we really want, isn't it,
to be able to commune with the unseen, the intangible, the incorp-

oreal and seemingly *not there*, to have those to whom you're calling out call back, for them to be ready with answers to all of your questions; in this day and age all the facts just hang there ripe for the plucking, you barely even have to reach out, and yet it's positively bizarre that the fact that Houdini was *not* the pioneer of the Aussie skies takes precedence over the other and related fact, the fact implied by the insertion of that devilish word "not," that he was beaten to the punch by someone else—and yet, strangely, it is this first fact that holds more weight than the second, than the one *vis à vis*, regarding, pertaining to who exactly *did* achieve this feat. Apparently it's more crucial to hang on to that miniscule but very weighty "not," that spanner in the works, that devil's trident of three letters, one, two, three, N O T: apparently it's better to know an enigmatic negation of a thing that never was, or that maybe was, or that was depending upon who you believed, or who paid the most money—ah, money—because you might also know that Erik Weisz, Ehrich Weiss, Harry Weiss, Harry Houdini was brought out to Australia *at enormous expense* by another Harry, one Harry Rickards, born Henry Benjamin Leete in England in 1843 before he left for Australia in 1871 to become a famous comedian, baritone and maestro of the stage who at one point owned and managed nearly every significant theatre, playhouse and opera hall in Australia, and was known as perhaps the most significant promoter, manager and proprietor in the world, the likes of which had never been seen, and who lured a host of distinguished performers from all over the globe to stages all over the Great Southern Land, not the least of whom was Houdini, Weiss, Weisz, who commanded a princely "Of the Skies" sum so exorbitant that Harry Rickards, Henry Benjamin, even noted it on the theatrical posters he printed to announce the series of flights Houdini would make in Sydney five weeks after his record-setting (depending who you asked) feat at Diggers Rest:

...IATION WEEK

——AT——

ROSEHILL RACECOURSE

MR. HARRY RICKARDS

At Enormous Expense Has Arranged with The

——GREAT——

HOUDINI

(The First Successful Aviator in Australia)

TO GIVE A SERIES OF PUBLIC FLIGHTS ON HIS VOISIN BI-PLANE

COMMENCING

MONDAY, APRIL 25

HOUDINI WILL

POSITIVELY FLY

BETWEEN THE HOURS OF 10 & 12 A.M.

Weather conditions after these hours being uncertain,

Flights between hours of 12 and 5 p.m. will be achieved, weather permitting

...DMISSION TO THE GROUND & GRAND STAND:

ONE SHILLING ONLY

70   The Swift Printing Co., Ltd., Jamieson Lane, Sydney.

And so the cost of getting the Hungarian-American to Australia became one of Harry Rickards' selling points, a trick still played by promoters and publicists the world over when they pay through the nose for something just so they can say they paid through the nose for it, because if someone knows you've paid through the nose, if they get the whiff of something big in the offing, you'll immediately pique their interest, which, with all the incredible noise buzzing around in everyone's ears these days, is usually a fool's errand, because how often does it occur that when one mouths into the void the void mouths back?, never!, not in my bitter experience anyway, but the ever-astute Harry, Henry, comedian and baritone and vaudeville promoter extraordinaire, knew the true value of the phrase "At Enormous Expense," which he put right at the top of his publicity material so that everyone knew the gravity of the situation, so that everyone got a sniff of the bigtime, this Harry Houdini was indeed an important visitor (as if they didn't already know, but "At Enormous Expense" no doubt sweetened the deal), in hope of setting tongues wagging, which undoubtedly had the desired effect—old Henry Benjamin knew how to gee-up a crowd—because nowadays it is indeed much more valuable, in an age when knowledge is not power so much as a license to speak, in fact it's not really even knowledge, to know that Harry Houdini, Erik Weisz, was not, did not, could not and now is not, than it is to know who in fact was, did, could and is. Because what matters, what carries the most caché—an invaluable commodity acquired often at enormous expense—is not what Harry Houdini did or did not do; is not that he was first, second, third or fourth; nor is it even *what* he was attempting to do—because isn't it true that many failures are indeed just as famous as successes, as it is in this case—nor is it even the fact of his defying gravity, because by the time he did it gravity had been defied already in every important corner of the world—indeed, he'd just done it himself in Hamburg (albeit to varying degrees of success, one of which included a significant crash)—but what really matters is the fact, and it is a fact, as verifiable as any other, that it was Harry Houdini, Erik Weisz, Ehrich Weiss, Harry Weiss, who did or did not do it. "Did you know," we can now say, "that on 18 March 1910, Harry Houdini, the man with the mesmerising eyes, the Hungarian-American who on arriving Stateside dropped the 'z' from his native surname—all the better to fit in or stand out—came all the way to Australia, at enormous expense to Harry Rickards, born Henry Benjamin Leete in Stratford, London, who, upon his death a year later in 1911, was survived by his second wife, Kattie, Kate, Roscow, Rickards, Leete, the Australian trapeze artist and theatre actor who also, in her younger years, performed as Katie Angel and was described as "the most beautiful trapeze performer in the world" as well as "the greatest wonder of the age!"—and is it any wonder, for high-flying acts never fail to strike awe into the audience's collective heart, their silver and white suits reflecting the searchlight as they soar overhead in defiance of gravity, in defiance of death and affirmation of life, arms outstretched, muscles taut, and if you look closely, if you have eagle vision, you'll see the blissful smile and sleepy eyes of the performer in a trance-like state as they enter the world of flight, as they cross a threshold and become, even if just for a second, superhuman, mystical, otherworldly; as they open a door to this other world so that we might poke our heads in and catch a glimpse of what lies beyond, a flash of the unbelievable, a flicker of the unimaginable, a flame of the seemingly unknowable lighting up the darkness, which is enough to throw open the door in one's own heart; I should know, it happened to me some dozen or so years ago when I first saw the woman who would become my wife, Alison, in a silver and red trapeze suit, flying through the air a dozen or so metres above me, cutting across the blue, red and yellow backdrop of the bigtop, colours swirling by, a kaleidoscopic image, and with the wisdom of second sight I knew that I would spend the rest of my life with her, that she would join my family's circus and we'd travel the world together and never be apart, living, working and playing together: a moment of clairvoyance that has proven both true and not true. No doubt it was a similar feeling to the one that came over the inveterate baritone, promotor and vaudeville proprietor Henry, Harry, Leete, Rickards when he first laid eyes on his Katie Angel wheeling, drifting and skyrocketing like a firework above him—yes, Kate Rickards, who would in 1921, long after the death of her husband, herself die of heatstroke while sailing back to Australia from England, in fact while crossing the Red Sea, and be given a sea burial, not before, of course, having mothered four children, three of whom had predeceased her, though the sole survivor, her daughter Madge Adelaide, only outlived her by some seven years, and had also been a singer and comedic actor in her youth, no doubt toeing the family line and indeed marrying another actor, a certain Frank Harwood (real name Joseph Gibbs) with whom she had a son, Harry Frank Broadbent, born Harry Frank Gibbs, who in turn duly changed his name when his mother divorced Joseph and married one John Allen Broadbent—although after the remarriage Madge Adelaide's son now preferred the handle Jim Broadbent—and who would also go on to become an aircraft pilot of some repute, entering countless air races and attempting to break many records, not the least of which was the England-to-Australia record—which he did, landing in Darwin after five days, four hours, twenty-one minutes—only to be lost at sea, like his dear old mum, like so many sons and mothers, wives and daughters, some thirty-six years after Madge, on 29 September 1958, when he disappeared in his aircraft, a Martin PBM Mariner, somewhere over the Atlantic approximately one hundred and fifty miles southwest of Lisbon, Portugal, along with his co-pilot, Thomas Rowell, four crew and thirty passengers—this poor Harry Gibbs, Jim Broadbent, was doubtless named after his pioneering grandfather Harry Rickards, Henry Benjamin Leete, who *at enormous expense* (£200 per week: the most any artist had been paid in Australia) brought another Harry, Houdini, Weiss, Weisz, to Australia in 1910 with the purpose of conducting the first ever controlled flight in Australian airspace, over an airfield, or rather a paddock (there were no airfields in those days—nobody knew what an airfield was!), a patch of dirt known as the old Plumpton paddock, at Diggers Rest, north of Melbourne, curiously close to today's Tullamarine Airport—must be something in the air out there—only for Houdini to be beaten to the punch and thus *not* become the first man to conduct a controlled flight in Australian airspace." Which is to say that it's more important, ie. carries more caché and is therefore a fact worth knowing, and not only knowing but repeating whenever and wherever one can, to know who, at the end of the day, it was that, at enormous expense to one Harry, Henry, Rickards, Leete, in fact did *not* conduct the first controlled flight in Australian airspace at Diggers Rest—which, incidentally, was founded along the road to the goldfields of Bendigo as a spot where the gold diggers could, you guessed it, rest—than it is to know who indeed *was* the first person to achieve this re-markable and hotly contested—though it was barely a contest, for Harry Rickards, who knew how to gee-up a crowd, had made sure that his publicity material spoke loud enough to put all other comers in the shade—feat. It's bizarre that the attempt, for it can never be labelled anything other than an attempt, because although Houdini did indeed, at 8.00am on that Friday morning in March, after a couple of initial attempts—attempts at *the* attempt—were thwarted by unfavourable winds, manage at last to achieve lift-off and forward thrust, thus circling round the paddock for something close to a minute and, for the moment, clinching the trophy ahead of rival aviator and competitor Ralph Coningsby Banks, who'd been trying to beat the escapologist to the punch, having camped out at Diggers

Rest in the weeks leading up to 18 March and had, in fact, made an attempt on 1 March in his Wright Model A Flyer only to travel around three hundred metres at a height of less than five metres before a sudden gust pitched him into the turf, creating an incredible impact that threw poor Banks clear and also wrecked his Flyer which then took weeks to repair, as did his confidence—his flight was not deemed eligible due to the fact, and it was a fact because the authorities saw it with their own eyes, that at no point in his three hundred metres was Banks ever *in control* of the Flyer—so that come the morning of 18 March, although his aircraft was almost repaired, his belief that he might beat the great escapologist to the title would never materialise, all he could do was stand and watch (and, incidentally and no doubt painfully—perhaps more so than the crash itself—be one of nine people to sign a witness statement attesting to the fact of Houdini's *successful* controlled flight) as the man with the mesmerising eyes, born Erik Weisz, the great entertainer who was there on a £200-a-week retainer—he didn't need it, but it was important to advertise that he was getting it—swooped in and snaffled the trophy, awarded by the newly formed Aerial League of Australia, recognising that his was the country's first controlled flight in a powered aircraft, when actually it was only an attempt, and this attempt, belated at that, would see him go down in the record books as *not* the first to have achieved the feat, but rather the second, and thus begs the question could it even be called an attempt, for a belated attempt to be the first at something could arguably be seen as simply wasting one's time, not to mention that of the nine witnesses, including the damaged and severely depressed Ralph Coningsby Banks, reporters, photographers (Houdini was ever the publicity hound) and, of course, a wickedly grinning, palm-rubbing Harry Rickards. In fact, it was likely that Rickards, Leete, the comic baritone and great proprietor of theatrical extravaganzas, who was at the pinnacle of his career as the most renowned vaudeville promoter in the world, some eighteen months before his sudden death in October 1911, had squashed all tell of the *other* first flight—promoters are prone to such deceptions—in order to drum up more publicity for Houdini's Australian tour, for both Harrys, Houdini and Rickards, knew not only how to work a crowd but also how to work the media, and being able to tell the newspapers that they would be able to tell their readers about the first ever controlled flight in Australian airspace guaranteed both newspaper sales and ticket sales, and indeed Rickards even made sure it was right there on the poster: THE FIRST SUCCESSFUL AVIATOR IN AUSTRALIA. So it's weird that the bankable fact that has come down through the ages, or rather the decades, over a century later, when getting on a plane costs much less than £200 and the only time aircraft appear in the media is when they are *not* in the sky—as I now know only too well—is *not* the same fact that was so bankable in 1910, is *not* that Harry Houdini was first, but that Harry Houdini was *not* first, a fact that seems more valuable now than its opposite was over one hundred years ago, and was why I, Arthur Bernard Cripp—though I go by Bernard because my father has already snaffled Arthur—have sought to recreate this particular controlled flight as opposed to the actual first flight, for not only did it capture my imagination arguably as much as it captured the imaginations of all and sundry in 1910, but there was also, as you'll see, a gravitas to Houdini's flight, the record, the facts, have all been held aloft by mere hot air, conjecture, hearsay and legend, which is to say that what I sought was to recreate not so much the flight itself, the mechanics of getting that old bird off the deck, but the idea of the flight, the hope of it, the *ghostliness* of it; and I guess that's also at heart why I am now writing it down, committing it to the page, once and for all, in no uncertain terms, in an attempt— let's call this an attempt as well—in an attempt to latch onto the idea, the concept "flight," to disappear into it, no, to *embody* it like the trapeze artist, in short to *become* flight; also to untangle every-thing, to make sense of it, to shout into the æther and have the æther shout back, to ask the question and receive the answer, the answer being the fate and whereabouts of my wife, Alison, and daughter, Beatrice, who—while I remained at home to run the family business now that Dad, Arthur, is increasingly incapacitated, on oxygen and in the grip of dementia—disappeared in an airplane (like the only son of Madge Adelaide, grandson of Harry Rickards, Harry Frank 'Jim' Broadbent), vanished without a trace, along with two hundred and thirty-seven other people, somewhere over Asia—possibly somewhere over Asia, no-one knows for sure—some six-and-a-half years ago, and some six years before I made my own attempt, my attempt at flight, out at Diggers Rest in a reconstructed Voisin biplane, one hundred and ten years after Houdini, according to sources at the time, especially that proprietor extraordinaire, that Peddler of Posters, Prince of Fliers, Harry Rickards, became THE FIRST SUCCESSFUL AVIATOR IN AUSTRALIA. Perhaps, I thought, when the idea for the project suddenly presented itself, as such ideas do—projects and wisdom, if ever they are to come, only ever come suddenly—perhaps I might understand something better, I might solve something, the riddle of the disappearance of my wife and child, the riddle of flight, the riddle of disappearances full stop, because as soon as the project suddenly, like wisdom, presented itself, the idea of parroting the Prince of the Air, the idea of re-constructing and recreating, in the most minute, subtle details, the most fiddly facts, for it is in the details where the truth always, without fail or exception, lies—one hundred and ten years later, it felt just possible that if I could shout into the æther the æther would, despite the fact that it almost never does, shout back; if I could go up in that rickety machine, defying the gravity of a century past—and we all know that gravity was far more insistent back then—even if just for a minute and covering barely three hundred metres, with nine people bearing witness, including a photographer and a journalist—like me, they would only be permitted to use the same equipment as their original pair, ie. a pad and pencil and a Kodak Brownie No. 2—I might have been able to find them up there, Alison and Beatrice, somewhere among the clouds, might have been able to call forth, conjure up, transport, a history now lost and in so doing perform a kind of time travel; which is to say that although I'd be going up in that antiquated, prehistoric, falling-apart contraption, I might also be going up in a kind of time machine, which in turn would mean that although the Prince of the Air, the Great Harry, Ehrich, Houdini, Weisz, was not the first person to successfully conduct a controlled flight in Australia, he just might have been the first person to conduct a controlled flight by a powered *time machine* in Australia; or maybe once again, despite his fame and fortune, despite his notoriety and acumen with the press, despite being backed by Harry Rickards—that is, having access to Harry's exceptionally deep pockets and vast net-works—despite everything both Harrys managed to get into the newspapers and onto the wireless, the Hungarian-American with the mesmerising eyes would once again come in second, because it would be only due to my actions, the actions of one Arthur Bernard Cripp, the fact of my recreation of Houdini's renowned though hardly record-breaking flight, that his French-made Voisin biplane would only now, in the twenty-first century, turn into a time machine, which would, sorry to say, dear Harrys, render *me*—Bernard to those who know me—the first man to travel back in time and beat the Great Houdini to the punch despite his having taken off from that paddock at Diggers Rest, half-an-hour north of Melbourne, one hundred and ten years prior. And so he would be second again, only by a whisker, but a whisker nonetheless, because while it was obvious that it would be me, Bernard, flying into the foreign land of the past, which was unbelievably closer than you might think, barely thirty metres over our heads, back to when journalists used a pencil and paper and photographers a Kodak Brownie No. 2, back to when witnesses to significant events signed statements of fact to prove that it all went down, if you'll excuse the pun, before the age of mass communication and instant messaging and shaky private videos of inhuman acts made public, posted for all the world to see, before the time, now, when every moment of every day is recorded, every statement, every slip, every trip to the shops, all logged and saved and cached and timestamped, before our time in which everything is evidence, in which we know and access everything, everywhere around the world, and a time before jumbo jets and their disappearances; while it's true to say that after building the Voisin and carting it up to Diggers Rest and taking to the skies, it would be me, Bernard Cripp, flinging myself into the past, it's also true to say that it would be the great Hungarian-American Ehrich Weiss, Harry Houdini, flinging himself *forward* into this, our, day and age, the third millennium, a time when we can barely be bothered filming the movements of aircraft at all, unless you have serious mental problems, because they have become—as everything does eventually, even grief—routine, dull, mundane, everyday, completely unremarkable. Which is bizarre, because now, in this pocket of time just waiting for the great escapologist to come zinging in scarf flapping, it is more or less—and more more than less— the unremarkable that is, in fact, recorded, filmed, saved, posted, archived and cached—meals, walks, dogs, cats, cleaning, driving, flowers, views, statues, clouds—while the miracle of flight, the absolute improbability, the *impossibility*, of something as heavy as, say, a three hundred-tonne Boeing 777-200ER ever getting off the ground let alone soaring at thirty thousand feet at almost 1000kph, is barely given the time of day and now comes in a very distant second to meals, walks, dogs, cats, cleaning, driving, flowers, views, statues, clouds; everything's upside-down, because we should be completely mesmerised by the fact—and it *is* a fact—of such an enormous contraption, the size of an office building, being able to lumber down a runway and hoick itself into the air with almost two hundred and forty souls onboard jetting off for the far corners of the globe. It's bizarre, even tragic, that the remarkable has become, in an age in which we're best equipped to share in it, unremarkable, in which the miraculous, three hundred tonnes at thirty thousand feet—imagine telling old Henry Leete!—has become so humdrum that we don't even bother monitoring every single second of every single instance of flight when truly we should be completely mesmerised; so humdrum that we don't sit around oohing and ahhing all day long like we did for the Moon Landing, as we should, watching out for absolutely every detail of it, as we could—why are we doing anything else?!—because the surveillance technology is most definitely there and would allow us to never miss a thing, not one moment, so we would have all the facts, nothing would be left to guesswork or imagination or likely or unlikely theories or suppositions and we could all say, "Ah, well *that* makes sense!" now that everything would be grounded in cold, hard fact. As I sit here writing this, I cannot believe my own eyes; cannot believe that I am not, this very minute, outside looking skyward—it's a beautiful clear winter's day, the air is fresh and even the sounds of the neighbourhood, power tools, barking dogs, passing cars, all seem so crisp and new—there's a flightpath on the northern horizon so I can see, every now and then, blinking lights by night or a glaring fuselage by day and really it's just astounding that I'm not online tracking every single flight in progress right this very second all around the world, shaking my head in disbelief and yet comforted by the facts, the coordinates, the waypoints, the messages transmitted through state-of-the-art fly-by-wire technology backwards and forwards to air traffic control—it is worth noting also that not ten days after Houdini's flight at Diggers Rest, George Taylor, who presented the great escapologist with a trophy from the newly formed Aerial League of Australia, transmitted the nation's very first military wireless signal on behalf of the Wireless Institute of Australia (founded one week before Harry H.'s flight, 11 March 1910)—those Kings of the Sky, whose eyes are, like a spider's, supposedly everywhere all the time, like the government's, so they tell us, there's no privacy anymore, the authorities know everything about us all, they have the facts about your age, date of birth, income, internet searches, habits, etc., they can compile dossiers on anyone they like, watertight character profiles, which enable them finally to lean back in their office chairs, clasp their hands over swelling junk-fed stomachs, and say, "Ah, well *that* makes sense!" Miraculous that I am *not* outside looking skyward like those nine spectators, including a journalist and photographer for *The Argus*, on that brisk morning of 18 March 1910, when King Edward VII, the "Uncle of Europe," was on the throne, though he wouldn't be much longer; less than two months remained of his life, which expired on 6 May, while he was in the company of his son, the Prince of Wales—soon to be King George V—who quietly told him that, that very afternoon, the king's horse, Witch of the Air, had won at Kempton Park, to which Edward, uttering his final words, said, eyes closed: "Yes, I have heard of it. I am very glad." What comfort the king must have taken in those facts, passed on to him by his heir apparent; you can hear it in his voice, which would have been gravelly if not outright ghostly on account of his having smoked at least twenty cigarettes and twelve cigars per day for most of his life and, throughout the preceding years, having suffered terribly from acute bronchitis, and so his last words, as Witch of the Air won and the King of England lost, would have been a very wheezy indeed "I am very glad," belying a comfort despite all his discomforts, the comfort no doubt of his greatest hope and son, the Prince of Wales, being by his side, but also the knowledge that his greatest hope of the racetrack had

17

come home first, as though the king's soul had already left his body and entered his horse's, metempsychosis they call it, filling his filly with all the might, bravado, confidence and majesty of the royal bloodline, the spirit of the age, thrusting her down the final straight amid a storm of applause and flashbulbs, under the gaze of hundreds and thousands of spectators craning their necks to bear witness to the final detail about this world that their monarch would ever hear, the last word fit for a king, "Your horse has come in," a manly king at that, twenty fags and twelve cigars a day, words that would give comfort and closure and a sense of life well-lived. Why do we not today watch the skies like those people watched Witch of the Air, sister to the three-year-old Vain Air, that day at Kempton Park in 1910, when the spectators, aware of the dire nature of their king's health, were unsure whether to cheer as they normally did when the monarch's horse came in first or otherwise remain silent out of solemn respect, and so emitted a sort of low foghorn blast of awe and wonder, both at the miracle of the win in the Sport of Kings against the loss of their king and the inner turmoil whipped up by these two conflicting events—it's such a bizarre, incredibly dazzling sensation feeling opposing emotions of equal force simultaneously—while arms were thrown around shoulders, ladies kissed gentlemen on their cheeks, all and sundry waved their hats, and yet the eyes were uncertain when looking over the grandstand as they did for confirmation of how they should best react, looking down as though already at the state funeral, looking up as though they might catch something high above? Why, when something can weigh three hundred tonnes and still rise thirty thousand feet into the air, why do we not stand there struck by the miraculous nature of the phenomenon, with awe and wonder, rendered mute by the joy of watching the impossible and at the same time by the fear the impossible arouses in us, something the philosopher Edmund Burke would have termed "awesome" long before the word entered the mouths of surfers and skateboarders; struck by the awesomeness of flight and noting down every single feature and facet of it, every fact, afraid to look, afraid to turn away? By recreating in detail, by scrounging up every feature and facet of that misbegotten flight of 8.00am on 18 March 1910, a Friday, a flight conducted by Harry Houdini, Ehrich Weiss, at great expense to Harry Rickards, Henry Leete, at Diggers Rest, north of Melbourne, in a French-designed Voisin biplane, with nine witnesses below, including a journalist and photographer, with King Edward VII on the throne—or, rather, in his sickbed—I, Arthur Bernard Cripp, Bernard to those who know me, would speak to the air and return to that age of awe, when there was still a sense of the impossible, when things occurred for the first time and not as a matter of routine, an age of wonder and consolation for life's crushing realities—because, really, our only consolation today is that there are crushing realities everywhere we look, we are not alone in our despair, in every direction, in every land, in every household, and so we're doubly crushed beneath the avalanche of crushing realities—when there was a sense of hope for what progress the future would bring and the world marvelled at what was possible, even though it all seemed completely *impossible*, which was what made it so marvellous, so mesmerising, that a man, albeit the Great Harry Houdini, at enormous expense, had sailed the great distance from Europe to Australia to conduct the nation's first ever controlled flight in a powered aircraft—an attempt that might not have been an attempt at all because it was belated and because the primary, essential and unequivocally paramount point of attempting to be the first is to ensure that no-one has beaten you to the punch—and that this man could, can you believe it?, fly himself up, up, up high above a paddock at Diggers Rest, completing a full circle and staying airborne for almost a full minute—how different everything looked up there, the vast flatness of this country, as far as the eye could see in all directions, a place of gigantic if colourless horizons, no wonder they'd had so much trouble with the unceasing winds, but also how peaceful it was to be away from everything down there, to be decoupled from that earthly existence, an existence that had become, for the Handcuff King, uncertain— before he landed safely on *terra firma* to cheers and applause from the nine spectators who ran up to him afterwards wanting to shake the hand not only of the Great Houdini but also the first (actually the second) man to conduct a controlled flight in a powered aircraft in Australia. All of which, of course, was more easily said than done; for, being as I was trained in fire performance, as a performer in my father's empire, Cripp's Circus—now solely mine—I still had no experience in flying apart from what I knew about trapeze, which I'd picked up from watching the ever-miraculous flights of my wife Alison, and therefore I needed to learn not only how to fly but also how to operate the vastly antiquated Voisin biplane, of which only sixty had ever been built, and which, although it became the second ever flying machine to conduct a successful controlled flight anywhere in Australia, had in fact been the first in the world to do so in a feat accomplished by a certain Henri (though sometimes Henry) Farman, the French aviator, when he held his Voisin aloft after taking off at Issy-les-Moulineaux on 10 November 1907 and completing a full circle overhead for a total of one minute and fourteen seconds, for which he received the Deutsch-Archdeacon Cup, and rightly so, since the Voisin biplane was less an airplane as we've come to know such craft and more like a winged bicycle upon which one sat as though actually riding a bicycle—its boxkite wings and skeleton providing next to zero protection for the pilot—which was why, at 5:14pm on 17 September 1908, in an aircraft somewhat similar to the Voisin, the American pilot Thomas Selfridge became the world's first aircrash fatality, when his Wright Flyer pitched nose-first into the Virginian soil at Fort Myer and threw him head-long into the wooden uprights of the framework whereupon he smashed his skull—and therefore was it any wonder they awarded Henri, Henry, Farman that trophy for going up like that, because to do so in those days was madness, sheer madness, or at least vigorously demonstrating what Freud would not all that much later term the "death drive" in 1920, a principle that was, curiously, first put forth in 1912 by one Sabina Spielrein in her paper 'Destruction as the Cause of Coming into Being.' So in making my preparations to recreate Houdini's flight, my attempt at his attempt at an attempt at a flight of record, it was imperative I learned the ropes and took my time—I'm usually a very impatient person, which is probably why I am and have always been so attracted to the fire performance to which I have devoted most of my life so far, the intensity of it all, the breathing, spitting, swallowing fire, or dancing with it, of holding it aloft and spinning it in the air, of walking through it, of setting myself ablaze; it is instantaneous, the heat the rush the spectacle, and the rewards are almost as unfathomable as the costs— and so after making several enquiries to local aviation clubs and the National Aviation Museum, as well as scrolling through the flaming comments sections of several relevant articles posted by the Museum of Applied Arts and Sciences—an experience one should have, but only once—I managed to track down a certain Francis 'Frank' or 'Southy' Southermore, a retired Englishman who'd spent his life working for National Rail between various hospitalisations owing to a weakened immune system and periods of alcoholism, and who with his wife Janice had relocated to Australia on doctor's orders that he take a long-earned rest in a warmer climate with more than a week of sunshine every year. Southy walked with a limp on account of a prosthetic leg below the knee, which meant he had a gait like a lurching top-heavy ship despite the fact that his false leg was of equal length to its biological other and had been fitted in England before his emigration by a doctor under the employ of the National Rail because not only was Francis Frank Southy (pronounced, of course, Suthy; rhymes with sully) in and out of hospital on account of an immune system that wasn't up to scratch, he was also prone to accidents and had, ten years before retirement, gotten his leg caught in the proverbial gap between train and station in such a way that the locomotive whipped it clean off just below the knee and saved the surgeon a lot of trouble, which was what Southy himself had told me—"Should've got a discount; I did half the bastard's work for him!"—when we first met on a cool autumn day at Essendon Airfield nearly twelve months before the original scheduled date of my time-travelling flight. The fact that Francis Southermore was not an aeronautical engineer—or an engineer of any sort, for that matter, his job at the National Rail having been that of a conductor for over forty years before he moved into administration, both occupations for which he was entirely apt given his painstaking attention to detail, an attention that at times bordered on pettiness, as for instance when he spent several months in my employ sourcing the exact aluminium sockets for the main frame and hinges for the ailerons of the Voisin biplane—this fact was of small concern to me; the blueprints were readily available from a contact of his at the Australian Vintage Aviation Society, which was soon to open a museum of its own, whose administrators initially expressed interest in joining forces to make my flight part of their opening celebrations, an idea I kiboshed immediately because their involvement was not part of Houdini's first (really second) controlled flight at Diggers Rest, and I told them in no uncertain terms that my project was to be as authentic as possible, which meant no more or less than nine spectators below, including a journalist with pad and pencil and a photographer carting around a Kodak Brownie No. 2, all dressed in coats and hats in the fashion of 1910, and all prepared to sign a witness statement of fact that it was I, Arthur Bernard Cripp, Bernard to those who know me, who'd taken to the skies at 8.00am that morning and thus recreated the first (really second) controlled flight by a powered aircraft in Australia, right there at Diggers Rest, built as a stopping place for gold miners heading to Bendigo in search of their fortunes, a resting place, a place to pause, a place of hope that you could feel in the air, brim full, like the hope before a great journey, no wonder they'd later built the airport at nearby Tullamarine, the whole area tingles with hope and optimism, even awe—it's truly bizarre there aren't scores of people out there just gazing up at the miracle of jumbo jets, three hundred tonnes of steel and plastic capable of achieving an elevation of thirty thousand feet—and so while I agreed with the Australian Vintage Aviation Society that the wonders of air travel ought to be preserved and people encouraged to appreciate them, mine was not the event through which great masses might again look up in awe unless you happened to be one of the lucky nine, and only nine, to be in that paddock at 8.00am on that particular morning. Still, despite my reticence to publicise the event, the Society was very helpful and managed to send Southy the full specifications, pages of documents and equations and numbers and instructions based on the original design for the biplane by the renowned aeronautical engineer and manufacturer Gabriel Voisin, whose machines are known today as the first successful aircraft in Europe (despite a few counterclaims) and who was responsible for the Blériot II, III and IV as well as countless Voisins including the Voisin III through X, a WWI machine sold to the Russians and used for extensive bombing raids and exploratory missions, all of which Southy explained to me between long oohs and ahhs as he sat on an unused aircraft tyre in a hangar at Essendon Airfield while rubbing the stub below his knee, which had begun to ache on account of the vast amount of walking we'd done—he took great pleasure in massaging that truncated limb and seemed to do it out of habit rather than necessity—inspecting the various light aircraft and looking into flight school. No, it did not faze me that Southy was no more an

aeronautical engineer than I—and I was certainly not of that per-
suasion, having been in and around circuses my entire life thanks
to the fact that my father, Arthur Keith Cripp, owned one of the largest in the country and my mother, Marigold Cripp, neé Hobsbawm,
helped to make it renowned through her performances as a celebrated contortionist, psychic and Australia's first female illusionist—
the fact of Southy's never having built a machine for flying was, to
me, merely a minor detail because not only was he the one person
who could build me the biplane in the requisite timeframe and for
the price I could afford—I ran a circus, not a bank—and not only
did we get along very well from the start—he was the sort of bloke
who'd talk to you as though you were his oldest friend, often starting as though picking up a previous conversation—but after me-
andering around Essendon Airfield—where we'd stood shoulder-
to-shoulder on the tarmac looking up at the grey sky as several light
planes circled above while he squinted, shielded his eyes from the
glare, and squeezed the makes of each model from the corner of his
mouth, Foxcon Terrier 200, Hummerchute, Jabiru J450—he then
welcomed me into his charcoal-coloured Saab, a car he'd owned,
so he said, since 1991, which had never missed a beat and was
practically bulletproof—he'd fitted a hand throttle and used his
uninjured left-foot for the brake—and took me to a large storage
shed not far from the airfield, beige roller doors as far as the eye
could see, his "home away from home," so he said, where he "lived
the life of a single man," by which he meant making aircraft as opposed to anything untoward, for his shed was full of scale models
of all different eras and sizes, some small enough to hold in your
hand, others almost large enough to accommodate a pilot, painted
in a variety of colours and made from a multitude of materials,
there must have been fifty or so in there—forty-six, he told me—
all in pristine condition and all parked according to make and
model as though waiting to be taken onto the runway and up into

the skies. Which was why I was not concerned that Francis Frank Southy Southermore was not an aeronautical engineer strictly speaking, given that he could recreate, from the technical drawings, an exact likeness of any aircraft—in fact, he told me he did not limit himself to such things; at home in his spare room (he and Janice had never had children) were all sorts of contraptions, trains and cars, military hardware including tanks, submarines and machine guns, and under the house, in what he called the rumpus room— I've always found people who live in suburban houses so odd—he had a model of the entire Melbourne CBD including the Yarra, which apparently took him almost a decade to complete, what with all his other projects, and which, he said with regret, would never be fully accurate given the changing nature of any city with buildings going up and coming down—an observation similarly put by my daughter, Beatrice, when we'd been driving through Melbourne and she'd asked me, "Dad, when will they be finished?" and I asked her, "When will they be finished what, darling?" and she'd pointed at the cranes overhead and said, "The city!" and I'd thought to myself at the time what cleverness there was in innocence—and it was something that clearly troubled Southy, too, for whenever he mentioned that particular model of the city his face arranged itself into an anguished expression as if a searing white light had abruptly emanated from the ground, or as if someone had begun to draw out one of his fingernails, and the fact that it still troubled him all these years on—he'd completed it almost fifteen years before we met—meant that the fact that he was not, strictly speaking, an aeronautical engineer did not trouble me in the slightest, especially standing there amid all those scaled-down aircraft he kept in storage near Tullamarine—there were some from the early twentieth century, though none with the boxtail I would require—where the smell of glue hung in the air, the light fizzed from overhead fluorescents, and those models seemed so real they might have fired up right then and there, ready for me, Prince of the Air, to climb aboard and take to the skies—which, of course, at that stage of my flying career, short though I knew it would be, I was in no position to take to the skies in anything because I would, over the ensuing months, need to learn how, beginning with the fundamentals of air travel, the theory, before moving on to practicalities and techniques, the facts, the laws, which in my most hesitant moments served to re-assure me—ie., there are indisputable, objective truths that hold the aircraft aloft, and bring it down, so everything will be a-okay as long as we respect them—and it was on those facts, those laws, that I focused during my intense year of reading and watching clips of and interviews with various pilots who described how a machine could begin jostling about, leaning this way and that—banking—riding out air pockets and sudden gusts, described as bumps in the road, and it was to them that I looked when the voice inside me sought to point out that this particular road was not, in fact, made of earth or bitumen but rather air, an element that in most other situations, except perhaps breathing, can be ignored completely, written off as nothing at all. Through flying, I told myself, I would ascend to the world of the unseen, a world in which the invisible was paramount and required care, attention and respect, but first, before I became lost in dreamy asides, before I became all haughty and intoxicated on the poetry of flight, I needed to learn how to do it, and so you could say that, standing there in Southy's "home away from home," where he'd already started tinkering away at some-thing over in that part of the shed that comprised his workshop, whistling a tune, surrounded by all those scale models, I myself was about as useless as every one of them, maybe even more useless; I myself was a scale model of a pilot at 1:1, a model of someone capable of climbing aboard and taking to the skies, someone who looked the part—by then I'd bought a bomber jacket and I've often been told I have a somewhat dashing "pilot" look, with the strong jaw and dreamy eyes, that windswept combination of manly capability and effete sensibility—though I was in truth someone who didn't know a stick shaker from an actuator and would undoubtedly, if required to jump aboard and take command, immediately crash and burn. It's bizarre to think that because of something someone did over a century ago—and not just any someone but the Great Houdini, Harry Weiss, Erik Weisz, Prince of the Skies, at enormous expense to another Harry, Harry Rickards, Henry Benjamin Leete, the great promotor, baritone and comedian, who'd brought the world-renowned escapologist out to Australia at the whopping-though-fitting sum of £200 a week, paid out from the day Houdini set foot on the boat in Europe to the day he set foot off it in Europe months later—it's bizarre to think that because of all this, because Henry Benjamin Leete, born in Stratford, London, in 1843, to Benjamin Halls Leete, an Egyptian Rails engineer, and Mary Leete (née Watkins), became Harry Rickards (partly no doubt on account of his puritanical parents' disapproval of his comic signing; they wanted him to be an engineer like his father) and had performed for, of all people, the Prince of Wales—who, as it happened, was Albert Edward at the time, the very same Albert Edward who would accede to the throne as Edward VII, the very same Edward VII who would, on his deathbed, receive news from his son, George Frederick Ernest Albert (by then himself the Prince of Wales), that his beloved horse, Witch of the Air, had won that day at Kempton Park, and reply, with his parting words, "Yes, I have heard of it. I am very glad"—so that that very same Albert Edward had with his own ears heard the baritone of Harry Rickards, had witnessed him on stage—the Prince's response to which is not recorded—it's bizarre to think that because Harry Rickards, born and bred an Englishman, had in 1871 travelled to Melbourne, Australia, of all places, and there found some success, as he had done in Sydney beforehand, and owing to money troubles had also toured America and South Africa before returning to the motherland where, particularly in villages and hamlets, he made his name as a "lion comique" and pantomime comedian, filling modest music halls and finding favour with "the provinces"—it's bizarre to think that this is perhaps why, in 1885, he returned to Australia, a.k.a. the Antipodes, a word meaning literally "having the feet opposite," presumably referring to the idea that those of us who dwell on the other side of the planet walk upside-down, and if that isn't a description of "the provinces" I don't know what is, Birmingham is one thing but Melbourne is altogether something else, and here he toured extensively with a vaudeville company to great acclaim, the Australians really loved him, and the feeling must have been mutual (and why wouldn't it?—when you find a place that loves you you love it right back) because after several successful years in the Great Southern Land, entertaining the crowds in capital and regional cities, Rickards took the plunge and bought the Garrick Theatre on Sydney's Castlereagh Street (a playhouse with a long history, even back then, of use as a vaudeville venue and had gone by various names including the Royal Marionette Theatre of Australia, the Royal Albert Theatre, Scandinavian Hall, Victoria Hall and the Academy of Music), changing its name to the Tivoli Theatre and opening its doors on 18 February 1893, until which point it had been officially closed for many years by the colonial architect at the time, kicking things off with the second run of *Mr Harry Rickards and his New Tivoli Minstrel & Speciality Company*, the first having been staged at the old Opera House in Sydney in 1892, a show that launched what became known as the Tivoli Circuit, an exceedingly popular touring company that managed to run for almost sixty years before being decimated by the advent of television in Australia in 1956, after which it lasted barely ten years because people were awestruck by the new machines they had in their very own living rooms, before which they sat and gazed in wonder at moving pictures to the catastrophic detriment of the once-beloved

Tivoli Circuit which was, like the great actors of the silent age, left behind by the march of progress and technology, having only lately been a raging success under the astute command of promotor, proprietor, comedian and baritone Harry Rickards, featuring ventriloquists, comedians, acrobats, trapeze artists, dancers and singers, travelling to Tivoli Theatres around the country including those in Melbourne, Adelaide, Brisbane and Perth—as I write this only one remains: Her Majesty's in Adelaide—and having boasted, some ten years after that first show at the old Opera House in Sydney, almost one thousand employees, all under the astute command of Harry Rickards whose puritanical parents would have been turning in their graves to know that their son had nicked off from the motherland to tour the provinces with a bunch of circus people— wearing a coat and hat, it's true, but also, when the mood took him, an enormous black tulle skirt that started somewhere up around his chest and brushed the boards like a fog on the banks of the Thames, these being the clothes of a man dressed for success and madness simultaneously who created an empire of his own, an empire large enough to attract the likes of Marie Lloyd, Peggy Pryde, Paul Cinquevalli, and Little Tich, not to mention the Great Houdini who would, on 18 March 1910, at enormous expense to Rickards, climb aboard his Voisin biplane and unleash a chain of events that would lead me, Arthur Bernard Cripp, to stand in that enormous shed near Tullamarine Airport over a century later and walk among those replica scale-model airplanes while their mastermind (though not technically an aeronautical engineer) whistled a tune at his workbench. To date, so Southy told me that afternoon, the largest replica he had built was—and he indicated with a kick of his prosthetic leg in the direction of the model in question—a 1:3 scale version of a 1915 German-designed Fokker E.III Eindecker fighter (actually, Fokker was Dutch but studied and worked in Germany), complete with Belgian linen covering, sourced from the same family business that had once supplied materials for the original run of two hundred and forty-nine aircraft—"The world's first real fighter," Southy said between melodies—which saw the hitherto wooden fuselage of machines such as Houdini's Voisin replaced with steel and a Fokker-Leimberger Gatling gun, capable of delivering over seven thousand rounds per minute, which was mounted in front of the pilot and which, via some very clever engineering, fired *through* the propeller blades, meaning that for accuracy the pilot had to aim the plane at his target, not just the gun, the implication being of course that the entire aircraft became the weapon, a machine of death, the firearm was merely the tip of the iceberg because what made the Gatling gun so effective was the aircraft's manoeuvrability with its steel fuselage, its wing warping for roll, its full-flying stab for pitch: it was an overall package which, in the hands of the right person, could wreak havoc on the enemy, and did, thanks to one Max Immelmann—who is often credited, mistakenly, as scoring the first aerial victory using a synchronised gun; a feat actually performed by fellow German ace Kurt Wintgens in a Fokker MK.5 (predecessor to the E.III) who in a subsequent letter said of the encounter: "I attacked at such a close distance that we looked each other into the face"—but it was Max Immelmann who, although beaten to the punch for the first shootdown, perfected the art of aerial combat to such a degree that his technique was immortalised in the adoption and dissemination of the Immelmann turn, a manoeuvre whereby the pilot flirts with the very limits of the machine's capabilities, spinning it around on the verge of a stall in order to swoop down on enemy aircraft multiple times over, a technique still in use today (though one I'd never dare attempt) if not in military aviation then certainly in aerobatics and air shows, and really it's the least the history books could do for the ill-fated German ace, for not only was he second to the first shootdown, he was also the second pilot to achieve the coveted six victories (here beaten to the punch by one Oswald Boelcke), which rendered him the second to receive the Royal House Order of Hohenzollern for the feat; but the eternal bridesmaid Immelmann would eventually tie the knot on 18 June 1916 when, after a (contested) seventeen victories, he was gunned down while flying over Lens in northern France by British second lieutenant G.R. McCubbin who, as (bad) luck would have it, opened fire just as Immelmann was executing another of his famous turns, whereon his damaged machine plunged to earth from a height of two thousand feet, making the pioneer ace the first of the three stars of the German skies to be killed in battle—the other two being, of course, Kurt Wintgens (died 25 September 1916) and Oswald Boelcke (died 28 October 1916)— while flying (in Immelmann's and Wintgens' cases) this very aircraft, this aircraft that Southy, while whistling, pointed at with his prosthesis in that storage shed at Tullamarine, not far from Diggers Rest. Of course, the E.III that I then wandered over to inspect, touching the wings of the others as I passed, was not *precisely* the same as those in which the German aces took their final plunges, for it was scaled down by a ratio of 1:3 and therefore, despite the necessarily diminutive stature of those early pilots, unable to accommodate anything other than a toddler or a little person—to whom, thanks to my line of work, now that Dad is in the final stage of dementia, I do have access (a little person, that is, not a toddler): namely, one Vasily Cosgrove, enormously talented performer, Cripp's Circus undefeated chess champion, towering intellect, formidable arm wrestler and expert drunk. If there was anyone who helped me through those difficult months and years following the disappearance of that Boeing 777-200ER from the skies somewhere over Asia, together with all two hundred and thirty-nine souls onboard, including my wife Alison and daughter Beatrice, it was Vazo the Terrible (his stage name both lending gravitas to his performance and nodding to his Russian roots) who offered no platitudes or clichés—being at odds with the bulk of the population means you tend to avoid clichés—and ensured a steady supply of inexpensive champagne, the circus being fully booked and constantly on the move, and who had me drive the both of us in my father's beloved opalescent maroon Jaguar XJ6 into the desert, once a week, so that we could scream at the stars till our eyes burst. I could easily have asked Vazo out to Southy's shed, had him climb into that scale-model E.III and sent him up at 8.00am on 18 March to complete a full circle of the paddock and recreate the second ever controlled flight of a powered aircraft over Australian soil, and undoubtedly Vazo the Terrible would have leapt at the opportunity, because not only was he exceedingly clever and physically powerful but he was also always on the lookout for new and increasingly devilish feats—much like the great escapologist himself—and yet it would not have been an authentic recreation, for on that crisp early morning in 1910 it was not after all a midget who clambered aboard a 1:3 scale model of a Dutch-German Fokker E.III Eindecker (not least because the E.III wasn't produced until 1915) but rather a 1:1 life-size original of the famous illusionist, stunt performer, vaudeville actor, businessman, scourge of fake spiritualists, Hungarian-born American Harry Houdini, Erik Weisz, Ehrich Weiss, or Harry Weiss, who clambered aboard the 1:1 French-designed Voisin biplane he'd shipped to Australia—having just flown the same aircraft in Hamburg (and reportedly paid USD \$5,000 for it) and now prepared to fly again on a retainer from Rickards of £200 per week (something to the tune of £24,000 in today's money, which alas I was unable to recreate!) from the moment he hopped on the ship in Europe to the moment he hopped off upon his return—and at 8.00am precisely took to the skies for something like a minute at a height of around one hundred feet above the old Plumpton paddock, with nine spectators, including a journalist with pad and paper and a photographer toting a Kodak Brownie No.2, looking to the heavens, and two disinterested horses looking down at the more appealing grass—another detail I wished to co-ordinate—which meant that to ask my esteemed friend Vazo the Terrible to jump into the already-built 1:3 scale model of the Fokker E.III would have been much the same as not performing the feat at all; the details would have been all wrong, the facts discarded, for it was an exercise in detail and fact, and if there was ever a time to stick to the facts it was in recreating history and taking to the skies: in both instances, you disregarded facts at your peril. And so in order to recreate Houdini's remarkable feat—that is, to be the first person to successfully and fully (there had been attempts before, minor ones) recreate the first (but really second) controlled flight of a powered aircraft above Australian soil, and in so doing to recreate exactly the image that appeared on page nine of *The Argus* on Monday, 21 March 1910, for that was the image seared into my mind,

and it was also the one against which I would be able to measure my success, for when my photojournalist got off his shot we'd be able to compare, to hold them side by side and say, "Yes!" and cheer or, "Ah," and be downcast like the two ponies, because it was an exact match I was chasing, anything less was unacceptable, it was all in the detail, the men would stand in coats and bowler hats, the ponies would be eating, as soon as I saw the image (which, admittedly, already looked like a stage set, such was Houdini's and Rickards' skill with the media) I knew that's what I needed—it was one thing to build the Voisin, to marshal together nine spectators in appropriate wardrobe out at the old Plumpton paddock, to climb aboard and take off and circle in the air for about three minutes and forty-five seconds while all below shouted "Hooray!" and "Watch the trees!" but that would have taken me only partway to my goal— it had to be precise, which is to say that just as Southy spent nearly every minute of his days at his shed at Tullamarine recreating versions of all sorts of machines, requiring patience, skill and fidelity to the tiniest detail, so too was I recreating a moment in time, an operation so delicate that the absence or abundance of a prop, a person, a horse, would destroy the entire endeavour and everything would fall apart, leaving me spiralling off into oblivion. It did not bother me in the slightest that Francis Frank Southy Southermore was not officially an aeronautical engineer, nor that he had never even tried to become accredited as such, for it was a rigorous approach to detail that mattered, and standing among his fleet of model classics, listening to him whistle as he tinkered at his workbench, I knew I had the right man for the job, I have always had a good sense for these things—I'm an excellent judge of character; you need to be when running a circus—because it was temperament that mattered most, and Southy's particular combination of earnest curiosity, obsession with detail, knowledge of aircraft history, lack of other employment, autodidacticism when it came to all things aeronautical, and the fact that, throughout the entire process, he never once asked me *why* I wanted to go through with such a project, nor did he ever say, unlike many others because these days facts are bountiful and there is nothing we cannot know, "You know that Houdini was, in fact, not the first but the *second* person to conduct a controlled flight of a powered aircraft in Australia," made him the right man for the job. Like Houdini to his stout, bristly, obsessive French mechanic, Antonio Brassac, I placed Southy on a retainer for the duration of the project—which originally was to be eleven months (though I paid him for twelve)—and, before we received the detailed plans of the Voisin via our contacts at the Australian Vintage Aviation Society, I'd told him that, for the sake of accuracy, it would have been best, seeing as though we were aiming for complete fidelity, if we could locate the whereabouts of the very aircraft Houdini had used in Australia—even if we had to travel to the other side of the world, we would have gone, *I'd* have gone, like Houdini did with his mechanic (at enormous expense, it must be said), and I'd have taken Southy with me to whatever corner of the globe in which it was housed—some collector must have it tucked away somewhere—only to discover that although following his Australian tour the famous escapologist had had his Voisin dismantled, packed up and shipped back to England, with the intention of flying it between cities on his next tour—a lovely little gimmick—his final flights in the Great Southern Land would be the last he undertook, for after being sent off from Australia his Voisin was never seen again—no-one, not collectors, not friends or family, not fellow aviators or historians know what became of that plane (presumably it arrived at its destination because there is no mention of it being lost at sea)—nobody knows what on earth became of that famous aircraft designed by the celebrated French aeronautical engineer, Gabriel Voisin, the creator of Europe's first heavier-than-air manned and controlled flight of a flying machine, which meant we didn't have that very same Voisin, with all its quirks and idiosyncrasies, its imperfections, tendencies, scuffs, chinks, dents, etc.—no doubt the stout Antonio Brassac, who, like Southy, had an eye for detail and an obsession for aircraft that bordered on fanaticism, and who barely slept a wink for months while in Australia, such was his commitment to Houdini's Voisin, which saw him tinkering away, assembling, disassembling, refining, tightening, tugging, testing, eyeballing and hammering at 4.00am most mornings, earlier when they were going up that day—no doubt Brassac would have fashioned his own solutions to problems that arose while in Australia, which meant that Houdini's Voisin would have been very particular indeed, for although Brassac had an encyclopaedic knowledge of the workings of the Voisin, the fact that he was so far from home, so far from the factory with all its specialised machines, parts and materials, meant that any problem encountered while in Australia had to be solved with whatever parts were available locally, and given that they would be in Melbourne for a month awaiting perfect weather—it is said Brassac (who spoke no English) was fond of looking to the sky and exclaiming "*Beaucoup de vent! Beaucoup de vent!*" throughout the entire month and thought Australia a hellish country to visit—and given the flimsiness of these early flying machines (especially compared to the almost indestructible ones we have today) and their propensity for being susceptible to gusts of wind, it was not inconceivable that Brassac would indeed be required to get very inventive when patching up wings, snapped struts, broken wheels and all the rest of it, and so the Voisin in which Houdini took to the skies above the old Plumpton paddock, after a couple of aborted attempts, would have been singular in construction, and if we were to get it absolutely right, if we were to construct the thing detail for detail in all its embellishments, for if it was worth doing it had to be done to the letter otherwise I might as well have just sent up Vazo the Terrible in one of Southy's scale models, which would've meant nothing, it would have been handy to have the selfsame machine (we say machine, but let's be honest, it was a boxkite with a motor!) available to us.

Luckily—and I say "luckily" because I am ever the optimist; despite everything, I still consider myself lucky, for the whole thing (ie. life, etc.) could have been a lot worse!—luckily, Houdini's visit was very well documented at the time; the media, whipped up no doubt by the efforts of promotor, proprietor and comic baritone extraordinaire, Harry Rickards, who took every opportunity to tell anyone who'd listen about the enormous expense to which Houdini's visit was putting him, the media was clambering over itself to get the latest on the famous escapologist's visit, plans, shows, thoughts on Australia, local intentions, would he be tossing himself into the Yarra, what did he eat for breakfast, because despite the great advances in technology—really, journalists don't have to ask these questions anymore because all you need to do is look it up, it's all there at our fingertips—the questions put to celebrities have been the same for the last hundred years and no doubt even longer (what's worse, the answers have remained the same too), which is to say that while Houdini's plane vanished after leaving Australia (in fact Houdini would never fly again, anywhere) there were still mountains of articles, interviews, reports, manuals, signed statements, books, photographs and testimonies to help us in our research, most of which had been digitised and scattered throughout the vastness of the internet—it was all there, all of history, and during my research I'd thought to myself that surely there was enough information out there that it could one day be synthesised in chronological order so that someone could read, in real time, the full history of everything, every event, every non-event, every drama and every boring Tuesday afternoon, all documented and digitised and included in the sprawling story of existence, minute by minute, day by day, year by year, mortality being the only thing standing in the path of the poor reader, for although this story would be practically infinite our time here is not, and while it's true that all stories end with death, in this case it would be the death of the hapless reader overcome by the sheer volume of words, the great black river of time, surging ever onwards, sweeping us all aside, or rather rolling us under like the Indonesian tsunami of 2004, or the Japanese tsunami of 2011, which by the way you could re-live moment by moment if you were able to stitch together all the footage from all the cameras, both private and public, and all the testimonies from all the witnesses, it's all there at your fingertips, stored not in "the cloud" as the marketing teams would have us believe—suggesting the information just vanishes before our very eyes while at the same time surviving somewhere in the æther—but in huge servers in both disclosed and undisclosed locations worldwide (the level of secrecy and security no doubt adding to the sense of nebulousness) including the Dalles, Oregon; Atlanta, Georgia; Reston, Virginia; Lenoir, North Carolina; and Moncks Cor-ner, South Carolina; as well as Eemshaven and Groningen in the Netherlands and Mons, Belgium, while it is believed that Google's Oceania Data Centre is located somewhere in Sydney (but nobody's talking), and those are just some of the ones we know about; no doubt storing the details of practically every moment in history requires the occupation great swathes of land (during my investi-gations I had asked myself why they didn't consolidate them onto those huge floating islands of plastic in the Pacific Ocean, known as the Pacific Trash Vortex or the Great Pacific Garbage Patch, for when I'd heard the word "islands" I'd imagined solid formations—perfect for building huge servers in which to store the planet's knowledge—but after a cursory search it became clear that these islands are not what they seem and in fact resemble more of a murky soup of microplastics, being thus completely useless) which is partly why, of course, we are asked to pay for storage of information, because the so-called cloud is not ephemeral or semi-translucent like the PTV—information doesn't disappear like magic into the æther—but actual bricks and mortar, fibres and optic cables and sensors and lights all talking to each other, it really is a worldwide web!, and if we could capture an image of it in operation, if we could stand far enough away to get it all in the frame at once—no doubt someone can do this; they've just photographed a black hole, for heaven's sake, using images from cameras positioned all around the globe and stitching them together—so that we could witness servers chatting together from one side of the planet to the other, firing things back and forth, sending on information from huge storage facilities to suburban homes (the term "download" is quite misleading because the information doesn't come *down* from anywhere; it's shot across the surface of the Earth and over the ocean floor), then I have no doubt it would resemble the activity of the human brain when viewed via a CT scan, with its hemispheres and lobes strobed by synaptic flashes, with its various regions communicating instantaneously—the amygdala looms large in my mind now, for in grief counselling it was mentioned over and again (I imagine it as a golden membrane, glowing and pulsing)—which is to say that in whatever we create, whether art or machine or business, whatever feat we deign to undertake, we humans cannot help but recreate ourselves, mimicking what we see around us and what we feel inside, even God, who supposedly created us in *his* own image, but that was because we created him in ours first, for it's precisely the sort of thing we mortals are wont to do (if the Great Houdini were to have called himself God of the Air he might indeed have had a point), so it's inevitable that when we stand back from our efforts and get a good look at what we've created, from the minutest miniature to a photograph of a black hole, from a wristwatch to the vast server network that comprises the internet, from Gauguin to the Pacific Trash Vortex, there we are again and again, which on one hand is a lovely idea, that the species cannot help but depict itself, but on the other is a trap, a labyrinth, and while we're often told that imagination will set us free, will sever the cord that ties us to the here and now and send us soaring into the clouds, there is, in the end, no such thing because any act of the mind is a regurgitation and perhaps the only way out of this maze is madness, for it is in madness that one can find relief from the bricks-and-mortar of the everyday—to lose one's mind is to float away, to drift up, up, up into the cloud of unknowing, the cloud of forgetting, unburdened by thought, rationale or history, drifting in the æther, lost, it's true, but blissfully lost, soulfully lost amid a haze of godliness, closer to god or nature or the universe or whatever it is that is too vast for our tiny brains—unphotographable regardless of how many powerful lenses you have in however many locations around the globe—which explains why the mad, the demented, the "touched" as they once called them, were said to be sacred, for they were the cloud, the perpetually awestruck and gobsmacked, belittled these days but formerly held in such high regard, for now knowledge is king, facts, details, the more you know the more correct you are, the more often you find yourself on the right side of things; but to be unburdened by the ever-compounding weight of information, to forget it all, to erase everything, for it to vanish right before our very eyes and to become God of the Air, how perfect—ridiculed and hidden away and even locked up, it's true, but how miraculous to make the ascent. Once again, Southy had his prosthetic to one side—actually up on the workbench (more than the limb, what struck me as incongruous was the way his shoes now stood in such odd relation to each other, one on his left foot as usual, the other on its side on the bench, laces dangling)—while he sat on a stool massaging the stump where his body ended and his artificial limb began, gazing up to the heavens with a look of sheer bliss, transcendence even, the expression of the mystic, the ecstatic visited, as his thick, calloused hands, which had felt like sandpaper when we'd met, like the abrasive flesh of a cat's tongue, and which, furthermore, were capable of delicacy and precision when it came to his work, when it came to tightening nuts and bolts just so, to pulling taut but not tight the Belgian linen used for the wings, to ensuring just the right tone to finishes, not to mention handling the minutiæ of his smaller models, the dabs of glue, tinier than teardrops; hands which now worked at that stump in a way that seemed to dissolve every skerrick of tension from his body, or at least briefly relieve him of whatever burden he carried around—his expression was a lot like the one, so I imagined, on the face of Houdini's mechanic, the pedantic Frenchman Antonio Brassac, as he circumambulated his beloved machine at 4.00am each day, scanning for imperfections, crouching and holding a lantern close, slapping at dust with a rag, testing joints, ensuring the lettering on the fuselage was clean and legible, retracing it in black paint if necessary and spelling out in well-spaced square font the name (one of the names) of his employer, whom he'd met for the first time in August 1909 at the First International Air Meet in Reims, France, at which Brassac won the inaugural mechanics' race in a Voisin owned by a certain Rougier, and the wily Houdini, wanting to fly but having no knowledge of how or even which machine to buy, surmised that, of everyone at the meet (reportedly, over the course of the week, there were more than half a million attendees), it would be the mechanics who would not try to fleece him; by January of the following year, not only did Houdini now have his own Voisin, which he'd picked up in Hamburg just before departing for Australia, but also the loyalty, companionship and fastidiousness (at enormous expense, it must be said) of the stout Frenchman who, for nearly a month after their arrival in the Great Southern Land, would wake at 4.00am, fuss over their machine in the dark, parked as it was underneath a tent in the old Plumpton paddock at Diggers Rest, where he would greet his master (arriving from Melbourne in his chauffeur-driven car) sometime between 6.00 and 7.00am with inevitable and unvarying cries of "*Beaucoup de vent! Beaucoup de vent!*" and a host of clever curses, in French (he didn't speak English), on this hellish place, not just the old Plumpton paddock but the entire country, of all places why here?!, it was so far from home—in fact, in 1904 Houdini had expressly ruled out ever travelling to Australia on account of the vast separation, "shouldst anything happen to my mother"; a reasonable concern, it must be said, for the anguish and torment of being kept from your loved ones by a tyrannical and unforgiving distance is enough to destroy even the strongest hearts and minds—and yet there he was in 1910, his mother very much alive and kicking in America, bothered not by the distance (which, if anything, was now part of the allure; it enabled such a cunning feat) but by the persistent and maddening winds that swept that paddock day in and day out, wreaking havoc on poor Antonio Brassac's nerves and causing him, every morning, following a step outside and a glance at the heavens, to remove the cap that was ever on his head and thrust it with great force towards the earth, muttering to himself "*Beaucoup de vent! Beaucoup de vent!*" and only increasing the volume as he saw the headlights of his master's automobile burrowing through the dawn gloom until he was prac-tically shouting at the great escapologist before he (Houdini) had even stepped out of the car when he (Brassac) would plead: "Why on earth bring us here to this goddamned *salope* of a place?!," even though he knew full well why they'd come: because at the end of the day it was a publicity stunt—perhaps they all were, perhaps everything the Handcuff King did was grist for the celebrity mill, but who was he (Brassac) to complain, given the salary he was on?— the whole thing was a publicity stunt, the quest to be the First Man to Achieve Controlled Flight of a Powered Machine in Australia— not France, not Britain, not America, but *Australia*, a place few ever thought about, the Antipodes, where people walked upside-down (needless to say, France, Britain and America had already been taken); he (Brassac) knew why they were here, because it was *bizarre*, and that was what his employer traded in, bizarreness, weirdness, the strange, even the occult, and what was weirder than the Australian bush?, which meant that he (Brassac) did not need to ask, nor did he want to cut short their trip on account of the princely sum he was being paid—in fact, afterwards, when promotor and proprietor extraordinaire Harry Rickards asked them to travel to Sydney (the record feat having been performed) to take the Voisin up at the Rosehill Racecourse, Houdini only had to whisper the figure he would add to his (Brassac's) purse for the Frenchman to commit to yet another month in that godforsaken place— and so even though he greeted Houdini every morning with armwaving cries of "*Beaucoup de vent! Beaucoup de vent!*" his suave employer (that handsome smile, that perfect hair) would place a hand on his shoulder and tell him patience, patience, *patience, mon cher Antonio*, for everything had to be just right, conditions had to be perfect, because in order for it to work, in order to get the title of being the first and thus the *publicité* for being the first, everything had to be perfect, the aircraft, the pilot, the mechanic, the weather, everything, "*Tout doit être parfait, Antonio,*" he said in his American-Hungarian accent. Because they'd seen, twice already, the results of everything not being *parfait*, both crashes being the result of unanticipated gusts, the first being mere days before they boarded ship in Marseilles to make the three-week journey to Australia, when they watched a pilot fly her Voisin directly into a tree, smashing it to pieces but escaping serious injury herself, while the second—and, for the two Harrys (Houdini and Rickards), the more concerning—had occurred not only in Australia but at the very same place, the old Plumpton paddock, where on 1 March, some seventeen days before Houdini himself would take to the skies, and right before his very eyes, an attempt was made to beat the great confounder to the punch and become the first to achieve a controlled flight in a powered aircraft in Australia, an attempt under-

written by a certain L.A. (Lawrence Arthur) 'Dicky' Adamson, then
schoolmaster of Melbourne's Wesley College—a quiet, portly,
"practical" Christian who owned a Wilbur Wright biplane (inheri-
tance had made him wealthy) and refused to allow an American to
take a prize that should rightly remain within the British Common-
wealth—"We'll have none of that," said Dicky over his morning
coffee upon reading in the *Argus* of the arrival of Houdini's Voisin
and its subsequent dispatch, on 24 February, out to Diggers Rest—
because, at heart, Dicky was a man of principle, one who believed
in King and Country, owing no doubt to his British birth and Ox-
ford education, he'd gone out to Australia on doctor's orders, for
Dicky suffered terribly from the pleurisy, and so it was advised that
he move to a warmer climate, and after he recognised that Sydney
was unacceptable (the humidity wreaked havoc on his lungs) he'd
made his way to Melbourne where, while waiting to be called to
the Bar (he'd been a lawyer by trade), he'd kept himself occupied by
teaching until finally, through a network of chance, opportunity,
luck and preparation, he found himself foregoing the law to edu-
cate young men, particularly in sports (back in England he'd been
a keen rugby player), having taken up the position of Sports Master
and playing an integral role in drafting the code for inter-school
athletics, the cornerstone of which was a principle of sportsmanship
whereby the boys would learn to "win decently and lose decently"
(a philosophy that would have done him no favours at the Bar), as
well as heading the Victorian Amateur Football Association and
working with the Victorian Cricket Association; all of which is to
say that Lawrence Arthur, who never married, was a man steeped
in competition, a man who lived and (in the right climate) breathed
it, who promoted pride and honour, so when he read about Houdini, this American (slash Hungarian), presuming to swoop in and
take the mantle for the first controlled flight of a powered aircraft
over Australian soil—and not forgetting that Dicky, as a man of

means, had a Wilbur Wright at his disposal, one he'd christened *Stella*—said, "We won't be having any of that," and duly called up his friend, a fellow Englishman, one Ralph C. Banks of Melbourne Motor Garage, who'd been in Australia just over three years—it is suggested that Ralph C. Banks was the given name of the performer/pilot who, following Houdini's tour of Australia, adopted the handle 'H.C. L'Oste Rolfe' (though Rolfe/Ralph never came clean about it despite the tell-tale 'C' which in both instances stood for Coningsby)—who had no flying experience to speak of, but who was more than willing to climb aboard Dicky's *Stella* in order to beat the haughty American to the punch, for there was no question of some hyped-up Yank magician who performed at children's parties taking a record that rightfully belonged to His Majesty King Edward VII, who'd been in poor health, it's true, with lung troubles of his own, and who would expire not long afterwards on taking a sort of Immelmann turn for the worse (the bronchitis that killed him was doubtless caused by his daily regimen of twenty cigarettes and twelve cigars)—on hearing about the King's ill health, Dicky had wondered if it wouldn't have been prudent for Edward to head south for warmer climes, which had done wonders for Dick—but wouldn't it have cheered the monarch to learn that a Brit, not a bloody Yank, had conducted the first ever controlled flight of a powered aircraft over Australian soil; wouldn't it have buoyed his spirits, maybe even perked him up a bit; who knows, a good mood is essential for good health, and so maybe good news from the colony would even get him back on his feet!, and how perfect too if it were to prompt a miraculous recovery in the King, some happy news that would restore him to full health—just imagine the Prince of Wales telling him quietly that one of Our Men, one Ralph C. Banks, had made the first flight in Australia and the King taking a big fresh lungful of Buckingham Palace air and saying, "Yes, I have heard of it. I am very glad"; it was right that it should be a Brit, and in a Wright Flyer too, there was poetry in that, Dicky knew it, Rolfe/ Ralph knew it, but the relentless Diggers Rest winds, however, did not know it, and so, early on the morning of 1 March 1910, a Tuesday, as Houdini was arriving at the old Plumpton paddock in his chauffeur-driven automobile, as Antonio Brassac was standing with one hand on his hip and the other holding aloft his faithful bandanna, which was producing quite the flutter, the Wright Flyer owned by L.A. 'Dicky' Adamson and piloted by the inexperienced but enthusiastic (and most importantly British) Ralph C. Banks/ H.C. L'Oste Rolfe ("L'Oste" being, perhaps, not the most auspicious *nom du pilote*) was trundling across the bumpy turf towards its unhappy fate; for the all-knowing, vastly experienced Brassac, watching his telltale bandanna, was already exclaiming "*Beaucoup de vent! Beaucoup de vent!*"; even when his famous employer sidled up beside him shaking his head and lamenting, "There goes the record," the wily, stout Frenchman knew better, and grinning ear-to-ear said once more, "*Beaucoup de vent!*" which prompted his master, Erik Weisz, Harry Houdini, to reach into his coat pocket and draw out a match—in those days, most pilots and mechanics relied on the "match test," whereby if the wind blew out the flame, you stayed on the ground—and he had barely struck his match before the incessant winds of that hellish paddock extinguished it, just like that, and so the foreign duo looked on with expressions of resigned entertainment as disaster loomed—of course, they did not wish any harm to poor old Ralph, but at the same time they were happy he wouldn't beat them to the punch—disaster which was not all that long in coming, for Banks' Wright Flyer had barely travelled one hundred metres at a height of just under five metres when a sudden gust sent the machine (they were known for being tricky to balance, and was the reason Houdini had gone with a Voisin, which featured a mechanism that balanced the plane automatically, a mechanism the Wright lacked) propeller-first into the dust, destroying it completely, tearing it to pieces and leaving only the motor and one wheel intact, which meant that that day, 1 March 1910, was indeed a day of miracles, not, much to Houdini's relief, the miracle of flight, but the miracle of Ralph C. Banks surviving that horrific crash, which saw him walk away with only a black eye, a split lip and a bruised ego, as well as a heavy heart knowing as he did that his chances of being the first to conduct a controlled flight of a powered machine over Australian soil were now shot to pieces, just like his (or rather Dicky's) aircraft, a heaviness doubled by the fact that he had not only failed in his attempt to take the record, but also that he had provided Houdini with an invaluable lesson that conditions had to be *absolutely perfect* before any attempt at successful aviation—that is, the match had to remain alight—and that if the record was ever to be his, if his feat was to go down, if you'll pardon the expression, in the annals of history (but more importantly to be printed on the front pages of the world's newspapers), both he and his French mechanic were in for a long wait. Still, I can imagine the look on Houdini's face as Banks trundled across the Plumpton paddock, sitting straight-backed as though trying to remain upright on a unicycle, running over fresh horse dung, rocks, branches, tussock, and then lifting ever so slightly when the ground dipped away, the tyres momentarily breaking contact with the turf, once, twice, three times, as he sensed he was becoming lighter than air, as the spell started to take hold, as the miracle began to happen; all the while Ehrich Weiss, Harry Houdini, watched on, his mesmerising eyes displaying a peculiar lustre that had as its ingredients part fear of losing the race into the skies and part excitement at the spectacle of flight, pure awe, a sort of innocence, a sense of wonder, and a bit of sadness—for without this new stunt, without the record, his career was beginning to stall—and it was that same expression that I saw in Southy's shed that day as he sat on a barrel with his prosthetic leg stashed on his workbench, massaging the stump just below the knee where the Watford Junction special had relieved him of his shin, ankle and foot at Hatch End station—which, in a way, was a boon because the insurance had not only covered all the medical costs (which, in Southy's opinion, shouldn't have amounted to all that much given the amputation had already been carried out by the 13:48), it also meant that Francis Southermore was no longer required to sing for his supper, his working days were over, which is to say that nothing is ever wholly bad or wholly good, and that curses can be blessings, and often are, and whenever Southy attended to the lump of flesh just below his knee I glimpsed that same look come over him, one that started as a wince but then changed as his thick, calloused, steady yet delicate hands worked their magic, changed to a sort of ecstatic religiosity, like those paintings of Saint Francis receiving the stigmata, part anguish, part bliss, part pain, part pleasure; we never spoke about it, but I did wonder at the time if he wasn't thankful for the loss, at least partially, for it had provided him with a great many happy things, a new life in the Australian sunshine away from grimy, gloomy, overpopulated London as well as a sensibility for the miraculous, the kind you don't see much anymore, and if you do, it tends to present as a form of madness. It's bizarre that we don't value the miraculous anymore, the strange, the inexplicable, the spiritual; it's bizarre that everything, even flight, even the mass storage of every spec of data under the sun, the complete sweep of history, has become banal in this age of information, humdrum, because really we should all be walking around agog, at the aircraft soaring overhead, at the messages on our phones beamed in from space or the bottom of the sea, at the faces on our computer screens; all these inventions that were aimed at making our time more our own, it's bizarre we don't just sit about marvelling at them; some do, it's true, but we view those people with suspicion, we lock them up, or manage to make the argument that they're involved in some sort of alternative lifestyle or they're the kind of folk who entertain conspiracy theories regarding who or what is controlling whom—I'm just as guilty as almost everyone, though I am trying to amend my sympathies for it is clear that the rate of conspiracy theories escalates in an environment where the governing forces act conspiratorially, which is to say that conspiracy theories are the domain of the powerless; is it any wonder that, for almost every significant event, there's an apparent explanation (if there is one) and a corresponding, complicated and more sinister explanation involving people and organisations and motives that seem, on the surface, completely unrelated, but it's tricky because while we acknowledge that making connections where there seem to be none is a sign of genius, we likewise acknowledge that it's also a sign of lunacy, and perhaps the real genius lies in the way the conspirators (if they exist) have convinced the rest of us to look with suspicion upon those who attempt to call them out, which is yet another conspiracy theory, one I admit to harbouring and one which has only just now, as I write, become clear to me: the conspirators conspire to co-ordinate certain events and catastrophes, but also, and more insidiously, they conspire to infiltrate the minds of the masses; to hijack an aeroplane in order to acquire leverage for a Latin American cartel that has ties to the White House is one thing, but to foster an entire mindset, a miasma of perspective and opinion, to crawl inside people's selves and influence the way they act, and the way they influence others, is the real black magic; that is hypnosis of the highest order, for even if we are to suddenly wake from our trance and suspect we've been led astray by the drip-feed of titbits and data, even if we step outside our established patterns of thought, in so doing we are stepping into a void where down is no longer down and up is no longer up, our bearings are completely shot, we are suddenly surrounded only by darkness, which is a terrifying situation, so terrifying that it feels safer, not to mention easier, to take another giant leap back into the safety of our established ways of thinking and forever shut out, eliminate, eradicate any voices that might try to convince us that there might indeed be other ways of thinking, other modes of thought. When my wife and daughter disappeared, there was no shortage of theories looking to explain how a Boeing 777-200ER could drop not only from the skies but also from all radar and radio contact in a world in which everything is monitored every second of every day, when they can find you whenever they want to, even when you don't have your phone in your pocket, when they can find where a pin drops; in an age when they can locate you at any hour of any day, and not only locate you, but list all of your tastes and habits and predilections and sleep patterns and internet usage and friends and relatives and classmates and whether you're having an affair and even what you are likely to do next; in an age in which there are such things as all-seeing all-knowing entities, but not of the miraculous godlike kind, more of the dull, mundane, techno hyper-surveilling kind, how can a jumbo jet—one of the heaviest things you can imagine—with two hundred and thirty-nine souls onboard, simply disappear into thin air? And that's what I mean by "conspiratorial": the authorities conspire to keep watch over us, to know our whereabouts at every moment, to be able, at the click of a button, to dig up our detailed, troubled, shameful, ragged histories, because now nothing is forgotten, ever, it is all there on those servers—even the fact that there are, or might be, *secret* servers, including perhaps one in Sydney somewhere, is enough to get some people thinking about conspiracies— yes, it is all there in that immense cloud of knowing; everything you've ever done and everything you will ever do is zipped up in a file somewhere, another lighter-than-air droplet in the almost endless cloudscape of lighter-than-air droplets making up the cloud, the dark weather pattern of all time, the unbreakable storm, it's all there brewing on the horizon—is it possible that one day, say a thousand years from now, servers will occupy every tract of land on the planet, both above and below the oceans; that Earth will, in the end, become nothing but a giant ball of information?—and given that, in our age of information, when any fact, datum or titbit is literally at our fingertips, we know this information is "out there," and that somehow we're adding to it minute-by-minute, hour-by-hour, given that we know it for a fact, is it any wonder, then, that our imaginations run wild to fill in the gaps in the knowledge; and given the nature and secrecy of data collection, is it any wonder we imagine sinister scenarios, that there is something cunning and even evil behind the unexplained, for in this age of freedom of information, why else would there be blind spots? what do they have to hide other than facts that are in their interest to keep from us? And so is it really any wonder that, following the disappearance of that Malaysian Airlines flight MH370 on 8 March 2014, with Alison and Beatrice and two hundred and thirty-seven other souls onboard, despite the fact that there are any number of highly sophisticated surveillance instruments following anything airborne at any one time, not to mention the many people tasked with keeping watch, and with the overwhelming volume of information available to everyone, not just the authorities, is it any wonder that, in the immediate aftermath of the disappearance, conspiracy theories flooded into the gaping jumbo-jet sized hole in our collective consciousness—a hole that was filled in the days and weeks afterward by yet more theories as yet more information floated to the surface, information that proved useless in finding the plane but useful in bolstering suspicions that there were things we weren't being told; and because, in those harrowing days and weeks and months and years, I wanted nothing more than an explanation, to know where Alison and Beatrice were, what had happened to them, so that I could somehow find them in my thoughts, picture them, even if what I pictured was horrific, I wanted to *know*, to exit purgatory, the darkest sort of limbo between knowing and forgetting, I wanted desperately to know where they were, even if it was somewhere I dared not imagine; because knowing had become all-consuming, because the *need* to know had become all-consuming (my therapist called it a craving for "closure"), I collected facts like rocks on a beach as if to use them to build some sort of sturdy and reliable shelter into which I could crawl and hide forever. The theories were manifold, often ludicrous, and difficult to keep up with, for they were intertwined with news reports, aviation authority reports, opinion pieces, grievances, doubts and accusations that only gathered intensity each time the word "disappearance" was uttered (which was every other sentence), so much so that I became swept up and submerged in an ever-rising wave of information, from mechanical failure to alien abduction, a continual stream of new theories, evolving ideas, new information, false information, statements and retracted statements, veiled statements and unreliable statements—at one point we all, all the relatives of the vanished passengers, received a text message (yes, a text message) from the Malaysian authorities that read: "We have to assume beyond any reasonable doubt that MH370 has been lost and that none of those on board survived," but they'd done themselves no favours in the believability stakes with all their "secret" information in the lead-up to this message, and so we took it with a grain of salt—which meant that, in my search for closure, I spent my days searching for clues, reading everything I could, disappearing down wormholes from which I wouldn't surface for God knows how long, absorbing not only the news and government reports but also conspiracy theory forums, Facebook pages, aviation handbooks, manufacturer websites, endless Wikipedia entries, one thing always leading to another, and another, and another, until I was completely lost and befuddled in a cloud of grief and data that didn't quite add up, my head bursting with facts and numbers and the laws of physics alongside all sorts of invented or supposed scenarios that included hijackings—two passengers were travelling under stolen passports—accidental shootdowns—the US Army has a base at Diego Garcia, which is vaguely in the area of the aircraft's flightpath—intentional shootdowns—authorised by the USA because the aircraft was secretly carrying a North Korean nuclear warhead—remote electronic hijacking—the aircraft's systems were taken over via software intentionally built into them—onboard electronic hijacking—the controls were commandeered by hijackers (maybe the two with the false passports) via a hatch in first-class that gave access to the aircraft's electronics and equipment bay—white collar crime—whereby a certain company that went by the name Freescale Semiconductor was behind the disappearance, for travelling onboard were the four other shareholders of a lucrative patent that would be approved just days later, thus giving Freescale full ownership—the "phantom cellphone theory"—whereby the mobile phones of the passengers would ring when their families called them, long after the plane was reported missing—fire—whereby the aircraft vanished because of a fire in the cockpit, landing gear, or cargo area, which led to a loss of control—"mass hypoxia event"—whereby everyone onboard, all passengers and crew, succumbed to the toxic smoke produced by one of the aforementioned fires, thus rendering the aircraft a ghost ship that flew by autopilot for hours before running out of fuel and pitching into the sea (of all theories, this is the one I most pray is correct, though "pray" might not be the correct word)—black hole—whereby the flight was swallowed up by a so-called primordial or small black hole that appeared somewhere over the Indian Ocean—meteor—which is self-explanatory—as are theories, publicly described as "physically improbable" and privately as "unhinged," relating to abduction by aliens, time travellers or "beings from another dimension"—to me, their absurdity, their recklessness and lack of sensitivity towards the surviving loved ones were as hurtful and infuriating as the conflicting messages we were getting from the authorities; and what's worse, the greater my anger, the more trapped inside of it I felt, and the strength of my inability to direct my rage towards anyone in particular thrust inwards while that very rage sought to thrust outwards. As for the flight-tracking data, the information we *do* possess, I here lay it out as I understand it (though "understand" might not be quite the right word): the aircraft took off from Kuala Lumpur International Airport at 00:42 local time heading for Beijing Capital International Airport, at which it was expected to arrive at 06:30 local time, which is to say that the aircraft was travelling in a north-north-easterly direction that would take it directly over Ho Chi Minh City in Vietnam and straight on to the Chinese capital, literally a straightforward flight path, nothing tricky or complex, up and then down without deviation; but that was not to be because, as the data records show, at 37m30sec into the flight, Lumpur Radar Air Traffic Control hands MH370 over to its colleagues at Ho Chi Minh whereon the captain issues his final radio message, "Goodnight. Malaysian three seven zero"—innocent enough at the time, even routine, collegial and friendly, but now chilling—and then, less than two minutes after this terminal communique, at 01:21:13, the flight's position symbol vanishes from the Kuala Lumpur Aerial Control Centre's radar, which means that for some reason the aircraft's transponder is no longer functioning, that is the ACC can't track it any longer, and yet the flight remains visible—a fact that is not brought to light until several days later—on Malaysian military radar, which shows that, at the very moment the plane disappears from the ACC radar, it makes a sharp left turn so that it is now, instead of bearing north-north-east, heading in a south-westerly direction,

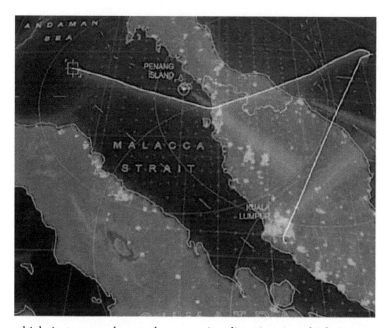

which is to say almost the opposite direction in which it was intended and back across Malaysia towards the Indian Ocean, and this is where it gets murky, where all the theories begin—Why did the aircraft disappear from civilian radar? Why did it make such an abrupt turn after its loss of contact? Was mechanical failure to blame, or was it something more calculated?—I want to be able to see them in my mind, to touch them, to be with them, to speak to them and have them speak back to me—it is at this point in the story of the disappearance of MH370 that my body becomes tense, my throat constricts, my pulse elevates, my stomach turns and I want to vomit; it's as though my entire being is trying to wring the truth out of the flotsam of facts, it's as if, if it tries hard enough, my mind will produce something to which I can cling; it is difficult to write this part of the story and I am in a lot of pain, and as though he can sense it, my father, who spends most of his time now in bed staring at the ceiling, has started moaning again and calling out as if in a dream;

he does this often and there's nothing I can do about it because he isn't asleep, it's not like I can simply go in there and wake him up; still, I go in and hold his hand and he asks who I am and I remind him and he says he remembers but I can see in those vacant blue eyes that he doesn't, there's only confusion and disorientation; I feed him stewed apple and he looks upon it as though it's an alien food-stuff before taking it from the spoon and the anger I feel at his in-dignity feeds the anger that has grown and taken up residence inside me like a twisted and thorned and carnivorous vine. I am back at my desk again; the writing is helpful; I feel like I'm getting close to something, or that I am close to something already, which is to say that it feels right to keep going, to keep getting my thoughts down, to keep riding the dark wave until it breaks, for break it must according to the laws of physics, which I have found to remain true in matters of metaphysics as well—because when something is true, it is true from all angles—I am writing this down to cut through to something, to achieve something like an explanation, an explana-tion of where I was and where I am and where I will be, a letter of sorts, a message in a bottle perhaps, and to be honest this sickly feeling I get whenever I come to this point in the story is a double-edged sword because, yes, my stomach wants to empty itself of its meagre contents but that is only because I feel so close to them, to Alison and Beatrice, sometimes when I write about my wife I can smell her, and so it is now, but I must breathe carefully, no sharp or protracted inhalations, no gluttony, no attempts to gulp down air, to ingest it all like Leviathan, to become God of the Air and carry it around in my belly, because the second I become too greedy is the second she vanishes again, each time as painful as the first, and so I have to breathe steadily, just like I learned in therapy, easy in, easy out, and that way she stays there, remains suspended, gently, gently, careful not to reach out and grab, like lessons you give a child, *gently, gently, don't snatch*, or when they're patting a pet, *gently, gently, no hitting*, and so I want to hold her there, of course

I do, but at the same time it is very painful to do so. Why did the aircraft make a turn like that, so suddenly and dramatically—reminiscent of the turn made famous by the German flying ace Max Immelmann, wherein the machine makes a complete about-face—

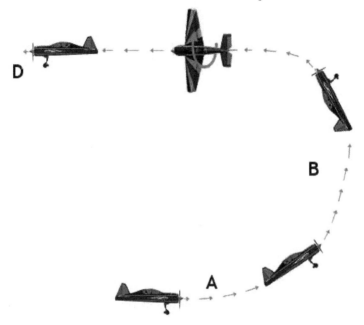

—immediately after disappearing from the watchful gaze of the Aerial Control Centre radar in Kuala Lumpur, for it is clear, and this is something we can all agree on, something we *do* all agree on, that these two events were not mutually exclusive, the transponder stopped working and the plane made an abrupt turn, two facts that lead inexorably to only two possibilities: either a) there was a mechanical failure (fire or software malfunction, for instance), resulting in both a loss of radar transmission and a loss of control of the direction of the aircraft, or b) somebody actively switched off the transponder and then, once out of view of the ACC, redirected the plane towards an alternative destination, which is to say that from these two observable facts (loss of transmission, rerouting of the machine)—if we call this the central point, *the thing we know for sure*—two probabilities emerge and begin spiralling around the core observables, and in turn these two probabilities create a wider spiral of almost countless possibilities including all of those I listed above and many, many more that are basically not worth recalling, for the wider out they spiral the more ludicrous and hurtful they become; still, each of the two probabilities (machine malfunction versus human intervention) raises questions of why and how, which is where we descend into chaos and everything becomes blurry or distant or like a washed-out echo chamber or like navigating an asteroid belt or the Pacific Trash Vortex at warp speed—or, in fact, everything becomes nothing at all, a great cloud of unknowing which is more like a black hole than anything else, sucking in every-thing, every fact, every thought, every idea, all light and hope; metaphorically speaking, if we take flight MH370 as a beacon of light and hope and, despite its absurdity, the black hole theory proves to be correct, then the image of the machine with all two hundred and thirty-nine souls onboard flying right into that sphere of darkness is, in a way, exactly what happened, which is to say that on one level the black hole theorists are right on the money, for the black hole is unknowing, or rather not knowing, a huge miasma of not knowing that extinguishes everything, swallows everything, all light and hope included—because in the absence of facts other than a and b—disappearance and turn—our imaginations rush into the void to make sense of events, even if what we come up with is finally nonsense, creating an ever-widening spiral of possibilities that is, and was, impossible to keep track of, despite my sleepless nights at the computer scrolling endlessly through endless websites. However, thanks to the Malaysian military radar, which no-one thought to look at at the time, or if they did they weren't speaking up, we do possess a few more facts, two of which might even be extremely significant, one being that the plane was now heading directly for Penang, the second being that the pilot, who was going through the emotional turbulence of a divorce, was born in Penang—two hard facts, irrefutable—added to which is the third fact that, whenever the nose of the plane deviated from the captain's island of origin, it was immediately redirected towards it, which happened time and time again, over and over as though someone was taking a long last look at home, for it is true that in times of chaos and uncertainty we take comfort in homely things, even when your home has been obliterated, things from your youth, even when they stand contra to your adult personality, you take refuge in the sounds and sights of childhood, which prompts the question: was the pilot saying goodbye, was he giving his existence the sort of narrative closure you can have in life but never in books, one last look at home, a salute, a tear and then goodbye forever, was the pilot giving one last wave to himself, his heritage, before plunging into the sea and leaving behind the loss and heartache and longing for death?—thus indulging the death drive and proving Dr Freud correct in his postulation—actually, Freud's the one who made it famous, but it was first postulated by Sabina Spielrein in her paper 'Destruction as the Cause of Coming into Being' in 1912, some eight years before Freud—and was he (the captain) in this way returning to an earlier, prenatal, inanimate state, not to mention taking with him the other two hundred and thirty-eight souls onboard, thereby rendering the disappearance of MH370 the deadliest ever incident involving a Boeing 777 and the deadliest ever Malaysian Airlines catastrophe, a fact eclipsed four months later when another Malaysian Airlines flight, MH17, from Amsterdam to Kuala Lumpur, was shot down over Ukraine and claimed the lives of all two hundred and ninety-eight passengers and crew, making *it* the most deadly incident the company had ever suffered as well as the second major catastrophe in a year? Was the captain of MH370 saying goodbye to life when he (if indeed the flight was under his command) pointed the nose of his aircraft repeatedly towards the little island of Penang, towards home, taking it all in and giving truth to Freud's claim regarding the competing drives in a person's time on Earth, perfectly illustrated via the metaphor of a pilot gazing at the island that gave him life while in the throes of orchestrating his own death, as well as the deaths of hundreds of others, because if we accept an interpretation of events based on certain facts—ie. his divorce, his place of birth, the likely mindset of the suicide, the last words, "Goodnight. Malaysian three seven zero," the deactivated transponder followed by the abrupt Immelmann-like turn—it all seems to fit together, but of course despite all these facts there is still no concrete proof, and if suicide was the mission, why did the aircraft make yet another turn, some thirty minutes after making the first, this time heading northwest from the southern tip of Penang and flying on over the Malacca Strait in the direction of the southern tip of India? Why didn't the captain complete the Freudian model and ditch the machine right there, right into the soil of Penang, and thus bring his affairs full circle, the opposing hands of life and death clasped together as one, he might even have picked out the very house he grew up in or the hospital he was born in, why commit to going on and not submit to gravity—for in gravity is death, hence the word "grave" in both its uses; and yet, here's Dr. Freud again, there is also the now antiquated term "gravid" once used to describe a pregnant woman, which is to say "with life"? Conversely, though, is there life to be found in death?—perhaps this long letter might go some way to making life out of despair, when all I have had is a wearying mix of confusion, numbness, grief and lies, maybe this, in the end, might be a ray of light in a dark and narrowing tunnel, an orange flare with the glow of a thousand million suns going up into the night, the spangle of starlight upon the ever-building black waves, if indeed there's light to be had; for that was not the end of it, in truth, flight MH370 did not end there over

Penang but instead continued tracking now in a north-westerly direction towards the southern tip of India until it was lost by radar some two hundred nautical miles northwest of Penang at 02:22, by which point several aviation authorities from Malaysia and Vietnam had tried to contact the aircraft, first via radio, then via satellite telephone, all to no avail—no-one was picking up—we do know, however, via a series of hourly automated "handshakes" between the aircraft and a satellite communications network, that the flight continued on for another 5hrs49min—during which time multiple ground-to-aircraft telephone calls were attempted—before, finally, at 09:15, it failed to respond to one final attempted handshake, thus extinguishing the last form of contact between the two hundred and thirty-nine passengers and crew and the rest of the world. Six years on from the disappearance, the most likely scenario we have, the one to which many from within the industry nod along and share glances, which has been teased out from a series of interviews and investigations by journalists and individuals often at a remove from official government channels, is that of the suicide of the pilot, an act that would not only rob another two hundred and thirty-eight people of their lives but would also cause untold pain and anguish to many others on the ground left waiting for their loved ones to come home, for just as grief comes in waves to the individual, it also pulses outwards from the centre like the ripples of a stone dropped in a pond or the soundings of a radar searching for a target or the spread of a contagion being passed from person to person, in this case one person's grief, that of Captain Zaharie Ahmad Shah, born 31 July 1961 in Penang, Malaysia, accepted as a cadet pilot at Malaysian Airlines in 1981, with which company he had remained ever since and by the time of the disappearance had amassed some 18,423 hours of flight experience as well as having been awarded a role as a Type Rating Instructor (TRI) and Type Rating Examiner (TRE) on the Boeing 777-200 fleet, by which means the captain was able to multiply his own grief and project it into the hearts of thousands of people around the world and in so doing not just end the lives of those onboard but also end the lives, as they knew them, of all others left behind. Which is to say that the likely scenario, about which the Malaysian government is keeping quiet, possibly in an attempt to save face amid a nightmare of errors, misjudgments, corruption and ineptitude, is that Zaharie is responsible for, after bidding Malaysian air traffic control goodnight, deactivating the tracking transponder at 01:21 just as the aircraft passed into Vietnamese airspace, and then, now invisible, making the abrupt turn to track southwest towards Penang—after studying the data, a member of an independent inquiry, an American by the name of Mike Exner, has concluded that at the time of the sharp turn towards Penang the aircraft was deliberately depressurised and simultaneously taken up to the dangerous altitude of 44,000 feet, which was not only above the aircraft's service ceiling (43,100 feet) but also would have quickened the deaths of all onboard, even with the oxygen masks raining down overhead, thus subduing any attempted resistance from passengers or crew whose air supply in any case is only good for about fifteen minutes. This would be altogether a turn of events that assumes the aircraft was now in the hands of one person, most likely Zaharie, more experienced by far than his co-pilot, for whom he was acting that day as Type Rating Instructor, the twenty-seven-year-old first officer Fariq Hamid, who had a fiancée and a whole life waiting for him back on *terra firma*, which means that by the time Zaharie took control Hamid was either dead or had been locked out of the cockpit—an easy enough task for Zaharie who could simply have asked him to go out and check on something specious, the cockpit being easily and impenetrably locked from the inside—thus allowing him (Zaharie) to fly the aircraft unmolested by anyone from either inside or outside, up to an altitude unsurvivable for those not equipped with one of the four pressurised oxygen masks located within easy reach of the main controls, which of course he would have by now fitted to himself in preparation for the rapid ascent while leaving everyone else to drift away due to a lack of oxygen—a process, so I have been told, which is horrific to us but was in all likelihood peaceful to those onboard, an experience not unlike going under a general anaesthetic, because the passengers would not have known much about the ascent, feeling a gentle shift in their body weight towards the backs of their seats, and would only have twigged that something might have been amiss when the masks, as programmed, dropped from the overhead compartment as the cabin pressure passed below a certain threshold: a moment of panic, perhaps, taken up by working out how to fit the masks, and then, with the crew telling everyone to keep calm, that everything was under control, to fit your own mask before helping others, a slow easing into sleep, a gentle loss of consciousness, no frenzied and desperate gasps for air, no coughing or spluttering, no cries of anguish but rather a fading of the volume of life, *peaceful* is the word the authorities use when they talk to us, though in the press they tend to use the more shocking and again hurtful word *asphyxiation* which connotes anything but a peaceful slumber, and so you will forgive me for deferring to the experts on this one, for if there is any hope in the matter, even beyond locating the wreckage and any voice recordings that would put all conjecture to bed, it is the hope that the passengers did indeed drift off to sleep without suffering, without melodrama, and despite Zaharie's deplorable and unforgivable act, it is hoped that he extended his people this mercy, which of course does not let him off the hook, not at all—if anything he was ascending in order to retain control of his objectives, not out of concern for anyone else!—but if true, and it does appear the most likely scenario, for there is evidence, thanks to Mike Exner, of the aircraft ascending to 44,000 feet, it does at least ease the burden of much more violent images while also providing us with a rationale behind the whole thing and that is, at least, *something*. All of which begs the question why—there will be several more whys to come, but the first is this—if we accept that Zaharie did indeed turn off the transponder, make the sudden turn and climb, and dispatch of, in one way or another, his first officer in order to steer the plane out to sea, undetected, on a suicide mission—in fact, in my opinion, regardless of the cause, any occurrence is always the captain's responsibility; harsh, maybe, but that is the way I feel; even if it is the other way round and it was, after all, the first officer who overpowered Zaharie and took control of the aircraft, the buck must stop with the more experienced man—then there must be a reason behind it, a sentiment that sprang up almost immediately on suspicion that the pilot might be at fault, a suspicion that has resulted in vast conjecture surrounding Zaharie's state of mind at the time as well as his psychological makeup in general; the official line, which most of us are less and less inclined to believe, is that he was beyond reproach and fully capable of getting the aircraft safely to its destination, for in the course of his career he had started, over thirty years before, as a second officer on a Fokker F27 before progressing over the next decade onto such machines as the Boeing 737-200, Airbus A300 B4, Fokker F50, Boeing 737-400, Airbus A330-300, and of course the ill-fated Boeing 777-200ER, racking up a total of 18,423 hours flying time, including some 8,659 hours in the Boeing 777-200, which equates to almost exactly an entire year of non-stop flight (a year being precisely 8,760 hours long); and moreover, so they have been quick to tell and remind us, in addition to all these hours in an actual cockpit, Zaharie was such an enthusiastic pilot that he'd had a full, sophisticated aviation simulator installed at his upmarket house in an upmarket gated community on the outskirts of Kuala Lumpur, where he would, much to his wife's displeasure, spend much of his downtime; but while his wife was evidently unhappy about his dedication, his employer, Malaysia's government-funded airline, was not, and celebrated Zaharie as one of their shining stars, such that their internal investigation revealed no signs of an inability to handle stress, no known history of apathy or irritability, no significant changes to his lifestyle, no family tensions, no signs of social isolation or changes of habits or interests, and after studying the CCTV footage of his arrival at the gate prior to the departure of MH370 they found him to be well-groomed, properly attired and showing no signs of anxiety, depression or distraction, nothing that would betray the terrible plot he was supposedly about to unfold; but in the face of the standard veneer of the commercial airline pilot offered up by the state authorities, there is another, darker image of Zaharie that has been pieced together by invested parties outside of official channels, for we live in an age in which it is virtually impossible to fly under the radar, for our histories, habits, predilections, obsessions, successes, failures, everything can be located by anyone who cares to look deeply enough, the age of anonymity has lapsed, especially for someone like Zaharie whose digital footprint was fairly sizeable indeed, comprising a YouTube channel, a Facebook account, and online career summaries as well as stored histories on all sorts of devices, the most important being his flight simulator which, after forensic examination by the Royal Malaysia Police, revealed around 2,700 coordinates that were deemed default positions programmed into the software he'd been using; but it also found seven manually programmed waypoints (entered specifically by the operator) stored in the Volume Shadow Information (VSI) file timestamped 03 February 2014, waypoints which, when joining the dots, produce a flight-path from Kuala Lumpur Airport over Penang, up the Malacca Strait, out into the Andaman Sea and southeast towards Antarctica,

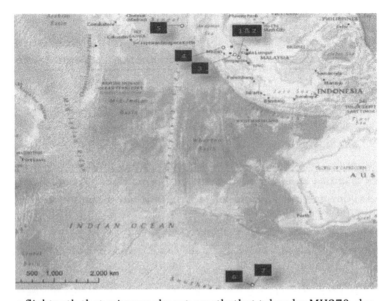

a flightpath that mirrors almost exactly that taken by MH370, despite which the Royal Malaysia Police Forensic Report concluded that there was nothing unusual in the data the investigators collected and that it was consistent with "game-related flight simulations," their explanation for the seven waypoints file being that it was impossible to tell, given the file's location and the way it had been assembled—a VSI file stores information when a computer is left idle for more than fifteen minutes—whether the coordinates belonged to a single simulation or several simulations unrelated to one another; and yet the evidence strikes me as starkly definitive—what are the chances of the data in this file being coincidental?—which is further compounded by the fact that it took the authorities over four years to release it. Then there is Zaharie's social media presence, specifically his Facebook account which, even as I write this, is maintained as what they refer to as a "memorialised account" whereby posts (presumably curated by whoever now has control of the login data) remain active so that people can visit in a manner similar to the way one might flip through a photo album or rest a hand on a headstone, making it a focal point for sentiment and longing, a chance to revisit the past and reconnect with someone we've lost, especially in cases where loved ones have simply vanished, which on the surface seems a logical and even touching thing to do; so Zaharie's memorialised account could be a place for a similar kind of reverence and reflection, revealing as it does a love of food and cooking, especially a particular time when he prepared a meal for friends or family prior to attending a wedding reception, featuring a spicy cheese ribbon, as well as breakfast noodles of shrimp and chicken the morning before the wedding "concorde"—a series of photographs which also features Zaharie cradling a bowl of uncooked mince in one hand while holding a glistening meat cleaver in the other and sporting a huge ironic grin—however, in concert, the photographs and comments that remain in Zaharie's account paint a picture that has raised more than a few suspicions in my mind; for starters, there's the fact that of the ninety-five photos in his memorialised page, in none does he feature with anybody else, this despite being a married man with three children; he appears in only five, of which two are selfies of him alone and three are of him in the kitchen (presumably taken by someone else), and only eleven are of other people (presumably taken by him): four on a day out with his model aeroplane, four with his model helicopter, and three of (perhaps) a few family members eating one of his meals, which is to say that in the three years of social media activity that remain attributed to the page (2012–2014) there are only three days in which he is shown in the company of others, there are no pictures of him with his wife or holding his children; in fact, most of the photographs relate to his "obsession" (his word) with technology, particularly rewiring, rebuilding and reprogramming computer systems, the pictures of one such project being contained in the album he titled RAMPAGE EXTREME: UPGRADING SIMULATOR—Rampage Extreme referring here

to the brand of motherboard he'd bought to make the upgrade—
to which, when asked by a friend (another captain at Malaysian
Airlines, it transpires) in the comments, "Z, how many GPUs do
you need to install?" Zaharie replies, in all caps, "DEPENDS ON HOW
MUCH IS ONES OBSESSION. ANYTHING CAN BE DONE FOR STARTERS. I AM AN
EXTREMIST SIM. HEHEH," which taken alone is not really all that
alarming given the name of the part he is using for the upgrade as
well as the word "SIM" that obviously refers to his love of simulators—at the time of the disappearance the media made much of
this "confession" while his friends and family rushed to Zaharie's
defence, citing it as an unfortunate coincidence, but when taken in
the context of the other supposed coincidence, the manually programmed waypoints in the retrieved simulator VSI file, the comment
acquires a more insidious tone. Almost half of the photographs
attributed to the memorial page are then devoted to his other
love, namely model remote-controlled aircraft, which appear in
over forty of the ninety-five images, two makes of helicopters and
his beloved radio-controlled model of a Consolidated PBY Catalina,
which in its heyday (1930s and 1940s) was one of the most widely
utilised seaplanes by military forces the world over because of its
exceptionally long range and effectiveness when it came to spott-
ing submarines and conducting sea rescues, most notably when a
PBY flown by Lieutenant Commander Adrian Marks of the US Navy
was used to rescue fifty-six crew of the sunk *Indianapolis* during
WWII whereon, when there was no more room inside the aircraft,
the remaining crew were fastened to the wings until they could be
transferred to rescue boats that arrived sometime later; Zaharie's
replica accounts for a large portion of the images on his memorial
page, from a day out on a lake with friends on 8 July 2012, with its
deep blue fuselage and primary yellow wings soaring through the air,
with large black lettering across the shoulders that reads "RESCUE,"
smog-tinted blue skies in the background, skimming across the
lake, flying barely three feet off the water, banking right and ulti-

mately splashing down and coming to rest on the calm, mirrored surface, smiles on the faces of those in the pictures (Zaharie himself is not shown); one image in particular has stayed with me, in which the aircraft faces away from the viewer having either just landed or gearing up for take-off, for the propeller seems to be churning up the water, the plane is in the middle of the lake with nothing else around it, and its proximity to movement gives a good sense of it being in action, of having been called to the scene, how it must have been when, on 30 July 1945, Lieutenant Commander Marks touched down at the scene of the scuttled *Indianapolis*, the word "RESCUE" practically leaping from the yellow background, and my imagination takes over, for I cannot help but replace the stricken US Navy vessel with the aircraft helmed by Zaharie and feel the strange uncanniness of this echo of displaced fate, a future that never was, a search and rescue that never was, the photograph of which appearing on the Facebook memorial page of the pilot of the aircraft that was sought but never rescued, and I cannot help but sense, in the context of other evidence, that this picture means something, explains something, admits to something, that it is a nod towards a fact, a truth, that cannot be included in any report and would not hold up before any magistrate, the language of the uncanny and the disturbing being not concrete enough to bring charges, yet it carries within it an access of truth, at the time a dark look into the future, now a revealing window to the past, a knowing wink from oblivion.

(Evidence of Zaharie's love for the Consolidated PBY Catalina does not end with his memorial page, for his YouTube username was catalinapby1; his personal channel is still active and features only five videos, one of which has to do with an icemaker and the other four with air conditioning, how to service and tune an air conditioning unit and how to maintain effective window seals; however, other than his keen interest in building and repairing electronic products, there is little to be found there other than strangers protesting his innocence based on how much of a nice guy he seems in the videos.) Then, leaving the photo albums behind, there's Zaharie's obsession with Malaysian politics, illustrated by countless posts made to his Facebook page during, in particular, 2013, in the lead-up to that year's national election on 5 May, an election that would go on to be shrouded in controversy when the incumbent right-wing Barisan Nasional led by Najib Razak won a second term despite the centre-left opposition Pakatan Rakyat led by Anwar Ibrahim outscoring the government in the popular vote, 50.87% to 47.38%, which sparked a lot of unrest, a number of significant protests, as well as a sentiment for many voters that democracy had been lost and replaced by corruption, a feeling that was only bolstered when, during his second term, Razak's security forces imprisoned Ibrahim on charges of sodomy and then faced charges of its own, charges of supposed sedition, all while being dogged by a scandal involving the state investment company 1Malaysia Development Berhad (1MDB); for anyone with an ounce of intelligence, including Zaharie, it was clear the country was being led by someone intent on running a protection racket for big business and a separatist regime that increased the gap between the rich and the poor, intentions that were revealed by Razak's implementation of a GST, suspension of two newspapers whose politics clashed with his own, and determination to bulldoze a bill through parliament that would grant him unprecedented powers; and the scepticism towards his government held by at least 50.87% of the Malaysian population would later be proven justifiable in 2018 when Razak was arrested by the Malaysian Anti-Corruption Commission and convicted by the High Court on several counts of abuse of power, money laundering and criminal breach of trust, making him the first Prime Minister of Malaysia to be convicted of corruption; it is a fact worth remembering that this was the government in charge when MH370, operated by the state-funded Malaysian Airlines, vanished into thin air with two hundred and thirty-nine souls aboard, and I cannot help but wonder how different things might have been if democracy had prevailed the day in 2013 when 50.87% of the population cast votes in favour of the opposition. Judging from his Facebook memorial page, this is a sentiment once shared by Zaharie himself, who posted with increasing frequency and fervour as 5 May approached, in favour of anti-authoritarianism and the more left-leaning politics of Anwar Ibrahim, for example making thirty-three posts on 28 April alone, between 20:19 and 22:58, and resuming hours later at 02:39 on the 29 April with another ten posts before 19:00, and again after the election, on 22 May, sharing pictures of the arrests of protestors supporting the activist Adam Adli and adding his own comment, "total failure of democracy," while comments attached to other posts include: "We r not going to be quiet," "there is a rebel in each and everyone of us.. let it out! dont waste your life on mundane life style. When is it enough?" and "enough is enough," as well as one on 4 May, the day before the election, encouraging people to "Vote wisely," reminding his readers that the futures of "our grandchildren" would rely on tomorrow's decision, pointing out his volunteer role as a vote-counting monitor, and apologising for any rude language he might have used (presumably) in earlier posts, signing off with "I am a normal human being who does not escape mistakes," all of which makes it clear that Zaharie Shah was anti-establishment, certainly anti-BN and -Razak—which, in a curious and perhaps revealing way, makes him anti- his employer—and maybe even a socialist with dreams of greater equality and a more sensitive, humane government, doing his part for a better future, refusing to lie down, refusing to be quiet; there is even the suggestion from several of his posts that he attended rallies, such as on 23 May: "see you there ... not for the faint hearted." Which begs the question: what would make such a seemingly compassionate person do such a thing?—a question whose answer begins with the nature of his social media footprint, for here was a man who, in his early fifties and with a wife and three children, apparently spent a great deal of his time alone, withdrawn, immersed in, obsessed with solitary pursuits, rebuilding simulators, rewiring appliances, constructing model aircraft, cooking, as well as posting almost continuously on Facebook, maintaining a page which attracted very little engagement from his modest cohort of friends, even those hobbies for which there are usually small but dedicated communities—I'm talking here about the radio-controlled planes—and attracted little attention even among his colleagues at the airline—curiously, for a captain of long standing and such vast experience, Zaharie sported few friends and followers; indeed, whereas fellow pilots within the same company have thousands of friends and followers, Zaharie had just over two hundred, and when he posted about his political ideas, or even when he put up pictures of his beloved Consolidated PBY Catalina, hardly anyone asked questions, made comments, offered compliments, so that what his Facebook memorial page offers us is, finally, a picture of an isolated soul, one perhaps whose solitude was compounded by his profession, for while the image of the international pilot is or at least was somewhat glamorous and gregarious, the reality is no doubt very different, somewhat similar I'd imagine to the life of the travelling performer, a life of aircraft and hotel rooms, liaisons with crew members (there has

72

been talk of several affairs with stewardesses), but otherwise bubbled off from the rest of the world, locked away at the front of the aircraft, entailing the use of entrances and exits separate from those of the passengers, riding in taxis or chauffeur-driven cars between airports and accommodations, at the controls, in command, with only an inexperienced junior first officer to whom you are a mentor, which is to say *above* everyone, not necessarily from an egotistical standpoint (though often that is the case) but just because that is the nature of the job, the hierarchy of the institution of flight, the tip of the pyramid, flight after flight, day after day, night after night, often with little more for company than the clouds. Following the disappearance of MH370, Zaharie's wife, confirming this image of the man, described him as increasingly withdrawn, their children were gone and living lives of their own, their marriage was breaking down, she had moved out of their primary residence and was living in their second house, and it was said by those who knew him that on days when he wasn't flying he'd pace the house from room to room waiting until he could go up again; until now, his life had been something he could control, the house was luxurious, located in a gated community, his hobbies and occupation were all about control, as were his politics and activism, and yet it had all spiralled out of his control, his family breaking away and fragmenting, the nation divided and under the influence of powers much greater than his own, the world increasingly at odds with the way he wanted it to be; in considering much of the evidence, mental health professionals suggested that Zaharie was clinically depressed, so that come early 2014, with so much out of his hands, there was just one thing he *could* control. The most recent photograph on Zaharie's memorial page, the last one he ever posted, dated 3 January 2014, just over two months before the disappearance of MH370, is a seemingly innocuous, low-quality, random picture of a movie being projected in 3D onto a white screen—

there's a shadow cast over a third of the screen, the shadow of someone carrying something, maybe a bowl of popcorn—an incidental shot, it almost looks like an accident, taken with the intent of alerting the viewer merely to the hardware being used for the projection, again highlighting a penchant for technology and gadgets—and Zaharie's caption reads: "avatar on xbmc atv2 panasonic 3d projector"; the film being projected is James Cameron's 2009 science fiction blockbuster *Avatar*, a tale of good versus evil with an ecological conscience telling of a future in which human intelligence can be transferred into another biological body—and the image is of the film's antagonist, Colonel Miles Quaritch, played by the silver-haired Stephen Lang, who is intent on exploiting the resources of a habitable moon on a distant planet without a thought for the destruction of its native population and landscape, a potent analogy for the kind of politics Zaharie himself loathed, Colonel Quaritch representing the right-wing, self-interested, corrupt and manipulative Malaysian government of Najib Razak that had won a second term in office ten months before, the government to which Zaharie was so staunchly, obsessively, opposed; primarily, however, it was the film's title that caught my attention—perhaps because it so closely resembled "aviator" and my mind was tuned in to searching for clues—and, again owing to my mindset at the time, I decided to look up the meaning of the word, having as I did only a vague sense of its definition, but being aware of its abundant use throughout the digital world. To my amazement—no, to my shock and despair—I found that, yes, the word "avatar" refers to a deity's incarnation in the here and now, but literally it also speaks to a concept of "descent," since the Sanskrit noun *avatāra* has its roots in *ava* (down) and *tṛ* (to cross over), while *avatar* itself, suggesting the embodiment of a deity in another form, also connotes "to overcome, to remove, to bring down, to cross something", and the verb *avatarana* in post-Vedic Hindu texts refers particularly to the "action of descending" without the spiritual allusion, while also carrying the double meaning of "laying down the burden of man," which burden is suffering caused by the forces of evil. It was bizarre, horrifying, nauseating to make this discovery, admittedly one which, in isolation, out of context, would be little more than a coincidence, an unhappy, unlucky, *unbelievable* coincidence, that the captain under suspicion of hijacking his own aircraft, dodging all radar and crashing it into the sea with two hundred and thirty-eight other people onboard might use this word, this image, this film, with all its attendant meanings, in his final act on social media seems both too neat and too impossible to carry any weight; and yet, in the context of the rest of it, the loneliness, anger, depression of Zaharie as his world came slowly apart, of the waypoints manually entered into the flight simulator, of the turns made by the doomed aircraft that could only have been made manually and not on autopilot, of the changes in altitude, of the model Consolidated PBY Catalina bobbing in the water with the word "RESCUE" across the wings, in the context of the loss of faith in the world he had built around himself, and in the wider world as well, the post with which he signed off featuring a scene from *Avatar* has folded up within it the force of truth, truth which, I am convinced, like a garden, wants only to thrive, to exist, to be seen, which is to say that even if Zaharie didn't know the Sanskrit roots of the title of the film he was projecting on that Panasonic 3D projector—and, I admit, why would he have?—there is a force, something like gravity, that draws things together, bringing seemingly disparate elements into harmony in order to reveal truth and explain the unexplainable and the seemingly impossible. That's not to say I'm left without questions—sometimes it feels as though all I have are questions—for example why, after the aircraft had vanished from all radar, after taking a long look at the island that brought him into the world, did Zaharie continue for another 7hrs23mins?—surely in that situation, you can't um and ah for seven-and-a-half hours, will I won't I, if you've got a mind to do it, you'll do it; talk to any negotiator and they'll tell you, if they haven't jumped after a few minutes chances are they won't jump at all, certainly not after 7hrs 23mins, not in most cases; of course, there have been instances of pilot suicide in the past, such as the 1997 Silkair Flight 185 from Jakarta to Singapore in which the captain supposedly disabled the black box before plunging the Boeing 737-300 into the Musi River in southern Sumatra, or the 1999 EgyptAir Flight 990 which was taken down into the Atlantic Ocean by the relief first officer, or the LAM Mozambique Airlines Flight 470, occurring only months before MH370, which was brought down deliberately by the captain halfway through its scheduled flight into the Bwabwata National Park in Namibia, and, who could forget, almost exactly a year after the disappearance of MH370, on 24 March 2015, when Germanwings Flight 9525, *en route* from Barcelona to Düsseldorf, was commandeered by psychotic-depressive co-pilot Andreas Lubitz, who locked his pilot outside the cockpit and descended into the southern face of the Tête du Travers in the French Alps, within the Massif des Trois-Évêchés, at a speed of over 700kph—which practically vaporised the entire aircraft—leaving a trail of debris over two square kilometres (approximately five hundred acres), and a trail of anguish all around the world and all the way back to Australia where two of its passengers had resided as well as many of us whose grief of twelve months before was exposed anew, in addition to over twenty officially recorded suicides by pilots of smaller aircraft where fatalities were limited either to the pilot himself or to a very small crew between 1972 and 2018; the primary difference between all of these and the case of MH370 is the amount of time between when the pilot began acting on a suicidal impulse and the actual destruction of the aircraft, for in all other instances the drama unfolded over a few short minutes, whereas in the case of

Captain Zaharie, following the abrupt and unscheduled southwestern turn towards Penang, there elapsed another seven or so hours before the aircraft stopped pinging the Inmarsat satellite communication network, which is to say that after disabling the onboard transponder, making the turn, donning his pressurised oxygen mask, and ascending to 44,000 feet, Zaharie then flew for between seven and eight hours completely alone, during which time he returned to an appropriate altitude, executed another abrupt turn (one that had to be made manually, not via autopilot) and headed out over the Indian Ocean as far from another human being as it's possible to be before eventually running out of fuel. I have asked myself repeatedly: Why?, yes, why do it at all?, but also why carry on for such a long time alone with nothing but (surely) doubt and guilt and terror clawing away at you like someone trapped in a well, why not get it over and done with and take it down right then and there, as soon as you're out over the sea? I asked myself over and again until, one night after waking from a short, unpleasant sleep, the answer materialised like a spectre in the doorway: to disappear forever and never be found; that was the *why* I'd been after all this time, and when I saw those manually entered co-ordinates from Zaharie's home simulator, it was clear that what the authorities had discovered were indeed the clues to unlocking the mystery; staring at us in tiny black rectangles were the breadcrumbs, the waypoints to oblivion; Zaharie wanted to disappear completely. Nevertheless, what does one *do* for all those hours after crossing the point of no return?—for a person who likes being in command perhaps it was an act of supreme control, mastering not only the aircraft and the fates of all onboard but also mastering his own fear and anxiousness to get it all over with, or perhaps letting the machine run out of fuel was a way of deferring blame and guilt, of saying it was not completely his fault, a gesture towards absolution; and while we're on the subject of fate and the questions that have gnawed away at my insides these past years—sometimes I feel as though I've dealt with them, put them to bed; sometimes I feel completely numb to it all, but then the smallest, seemingly insignificant thing, a word on a billboard, a scarf in a window, a child's scream, will cause me such incredible pain that for a moment, sometimes longer, I am unable to breathe and I stand there pulverised, choking on my own grief; but questions still arise and it seems there is now no living without them, the story of my life, of who I am, has become the questions of my life and who I am, instead of being anchored to bedrock statements I am now enveloped in a haze of questions and the chaos of my own mind; for instance why had Alison and Beatrice stopped in Malaysia first before Beijing, when the trip could easily have been done in the reverse?—they had visited the Zoo Negara in Kuala Lumpur where they looked at a twenty-three-year-old Borneo elephant to include in Cripp's Circus, and were heading for Beijing Zoo where they were to look at a six-year-old South China tiger; we'd all been to China before only four years earlier for a similar purpose, but because of my father's deteriorating health, as well as the rareness of the opportunity to acquire these particular animals, it was decided that I would stay at home to look after Dad and the girls would do something special together; Beatrice was climbing the walls with excitement at the prospect of spending two weeks visiting zoos and being around exotic animals, it was something she'd taken to naturally and wholeheartedly; whenever we wondered where she was, we knew we'd find her by the animal trailers talking to the monkeys or Dedalus the donkey or Iago the lion, or trying to convince old Pinky McCubbin, our animal trainer, to let her ride one of the horses (he could never refuse; she had him under her spell), which she did daily without fail and it was clear that she'd inherited from her mother an affinity with all species, including humans, both of them had an eye for temperament; ever since my father's retirement,

Alison had taken over the management of the animals, and it was to her judgement that I always deferred, which was the reason why, in addition to Dad's condition, she was going and I was staying home. After the plane they were travelling on disappeared it was as though I had disappeared, I couldn't eat or sleep, I couldn't sit still, I had to, for some reason, keep moving, pacing the house, walking around the block, but I was so tired and malnourished I sometimes couldn't make it home; the only thing I had in spades were questions: all the questions to do with the aircraft's pilot, his state of mind and the mysterious and horrific execution of his suicide mission, yes, but also those questions to do with the girls' trip; the most immediate being why wasn't I with them, why couldn't I have gone down with them, for in the days and months following the disappearance it was all I wanted; why couldn't we have had a nurse look after Dad?—it is a question that, despite the therapy and the things I've learned to say to myself, persists even now—why couldn't I have died too? In a way I blamed Dad; why did he have to succumb to the onset of dementia, why was he forgetting faces, names, appointments, birthdays, anniversaries, and why *then*, why not a year later?—and the most bitter reality was that, following the disappearance, I had to get a nurse in to take care of Dad anyway because I was in no fit state to look after myself let alone anyone else; and why could they not have gone to see the South China tiger in Beijing first; who had made that decision to travel via Kuala Lumpur, the travel agent?—the *travel agent*, for God's sake, decided our fate; why could they not have taken an earlier flight or the next day's flight; of all the services and airlines, why that one in particular; why couldn't the taxi have broken down on the way to the airport or missed the turn-off or become stuck in traffic; why couldn't I have called and prevented them from leaving on time; why couldn't they have forgotten something back at the hotel, their passports, a credit card, a wedding ring; why had I taken over that damned circus, which was becoming less popular with every tour and had been in a steady decline ever since my grandfather passed it on to my father in the mid-1960s, when the advent of television had caused a huge drop in audience numbers, why hadn't we shut it down then and entered the workforce like a normal family, why did we need Borneo elephants and South China tigers when awe and wonder were already things of the past? All I was left with were questions, the hazy ephemera of askance, a dizzying vortex of half-recalled facts and half-baked theories, without the gravity of an answer, without the voices of my wife and daughter for ballast, without the purpose, direction, focus and groundedness they had given to my existence; they were gone, and what's more there was no evidence of where they had gone to, nothing tangible to tell us what had happened, no point on a map to say that *this* is where they came to rest, no letter from Zaharie to explain what he'd done and why, no voice recording, no coded message, not even a hint on his face in the CCTV footage of his arrival at the departure gate that might tell us what was on his mind, nothing at all, I am lost in a fog. The last time I spoke with them they'd just returned to their hotel having visited Sabah the elephant for the third day in a row, not only on account of Beatrice's enthusiasm but in order to see how Sabah responded to them as they became familiar with him; they were both excited, Alison was trying to negotiate a price because the Malaysians were asking a lot of money, but she was convinced they'd come to an agreement in the next few days; they were leaving Kuala Lumpur that night, there was a future, there was meaning, there was (apparent) certainty or at least a direction; they would call once settled in their next hotel; and then nothing, no explanation, no co-ordinates, no remains, no goodbyes, nothing; I reached out and grabbed only air, reached out for something solid but seized only questions. It's bizarre that the phrase "to pull a Houdini" has come to mean "to disappear," because that is not what the Great Harry, Ehrich Weiss, was known for; if anything, he became known for the exact opposite of disappearing, *re*appearing as he did after being locked up in all sorts of restraints such as handcuffs, ropes, chains and straightjackets, as well as being locked inside spaces like prison cells, water-filled tanks, packing crates, boilers that had been riveted shut, beer-filled barrels and even, on one occasion, the belly of a "freak sea monster" that had washed up on a Boston beach in 1911, which was remarkable not only because of the challenge's novelty or bizarreness, nor because nearly all of his escapes were in themselves remarkable, but because of the monster itself (there was much debate about what it actually was: some thought it a seal, others a whale, while Houdini described it as a "mongrel breed of whale and octopus"—but from the surviving image it seems to have been a giant leatherback turtle), since after it was rolled out on stage at Boston's B.F. Keith's Theatre, and the cunning escapologist, with great difficulty, had climbed inside, the creature was sewn up and wrapped in chains looped through metal eyelets some three inches apart and held together by a series of padlocks that surely rattled and clanked as Houdini plied his trade, making the creature look like it was in the throes of giving birth, everyone must have been holding their breath—there are no accounts of any stench from the creature, probably due to the fact that one of the men behind the challenge (it was reported that ten "businessmen" conjured up the idea) was a taxidermist and thus versed in the preparation and preservation of corpses—and so the whole auditorium, "choked to the doors," sat breathless out of fear and awe for fifteen minutes waiting for the emergence of the hero— there was always the threat of death back then, who deals in death these days, I wonder; hardly anyone; death as entertainment has shifted to another sphere—who did indeed, at last, appear, *re*appear, covered no doubt in all manner of viscera and sea-creature fluids, his hair slicked with it, gasping for air but still smiling and waving to his adoring fans—what no-one realised at the time, how could they?, was that the Great Illusionist had almost succumbed to arsenic poisoning from the embalming fluids, though even if they knew nothing of the arsenic, they nevertheless sensed that it was a death-defying stunt—not to mention the sheer visual spectacle of it all—the thrill of which reached its zenith with the reappearance on stage of Houdini, covered in muck, dizzy and nauseous, who in the days following, the press likened to Jonah freed from the innards of the whale, another great reappearer, but whereas Jonah took three days to come back (and some in turn liken Jonah to Jesus, and the whale story as a precursor to that of the return of God's son; we are steeped in stories of reappearance) it only took Houdini fifteen minutes to complete a challenge that would go down, even to the famous escapologist himself, as one of his most significant efforts, the key to its success being, of course, his reappearance on stage, for that was the moment that brought the house down and added another chapter to the growing myth of the man from Hungary who held everyone in a state of disbelief. All of which is to say that to use the name Houdini to refer to a disappearing or vanishing act is misleading, for that was not what he did, that was only half the story; he returned; he came back, he escaped death, outwitted oblivion, and so when some commentator or other made the offhand and particularly hurtful remark that MH370 had "pulled a Houdini," it was clear that they did not know what they were talking about, because if it *had* pulled a Houdini, which was what we were all praying for, it would have reappeared, it would have come back to us, Alison and Beatrice would have returned home, but that's not what happened because in reality after making its Immelmann-like turn towards the Indian Ocean followed by a couple of additional minor turns, it dropped off all radar and vanished without a trace, without a signal, without a call for help, a mayday, nothing, gone forever, Jonah swallowed by the whale and

82

never making it out—of all the crazy theories, I'm yet to come across one arguing for the Leviathan, though doubtless it's out there—vanished like the poor wife of the great promotor, vaudeville proprietor, comic baritone and theatre owner Harry Rickards, Kate Rickards ("Katie Angel" as she was known during her trapeze artist years, who soared against the blue, red and yellow of the bigtop and captured the hearts and minds not only of the audience, but of old Henry Leete, Harry Rickards, who must have stood agog at the Flying Woman and said to himself, "Yes, that's the woman of my heart," I know the feeling, Harry, I know it well, for I too have stood as you did, arms slack by my sides, gazing up at my own Flying Woman, though Alison went by The Amazing Aerialist Antoinette), poor Katie, who was buried somewhere in the Red Sea after succumbing to heatstroke in 1922, eleven years after the death of her husband, *en route* to Australia from England; vanished like her grandson, Harry Frank 'Jim' Broadbent, who in 1958, after a distinguished flying career including a record-breaking flight between England and Australia in 1938, together with his co-pilot, four crew and thirty passengers, vanished over the Atlantic Ocean one hundred and fifty miles southwest of Lisbon, never to be seen or heard from again; vanished like that national icon, barnstormer, face of the lobster-coloured twenty dollar note, Sir Charles Kingsford Smith, 'Smithy' to his friends (and later the entire nation), first to conduct the transpacific flight from the USA to Australia in a Fokker F.VII named *Lady Southern Cross*, first to conduct a nonstop crossing of the Australian mainland, who in 1935, in an attempt to break the England-to-Australia record, during the India-to-Singapore leg of the flight, disappeared somewhere over the Andaman Sea, the same sea, so it happens, over which MH370 vanished from Malaysian military radar without a trace, a fact that seemed laden with promise when I first observed it—could the disappearance of both machines help provide an explanation for each?—but one that has, in the end, produced nothing but the silence of the wide-open and untrammelled seas. In fact, the term "without a trace" is not quite accurate in either circumstance, neither Smithy's nor in the case of MH370, for some eighteen months after the disappearance of Kingsford Smith, a Burmese fisherman found a leg and wheel (still inflated) that washed up on the shore of Aye Island not far off the Burma coast and was later identified by experts as belonging to the *Lady Southern Cross*, Smithy's doomed aircraft; likewise, some sixteen months after its disappearance, someone happened upon a part of a wing on a beach on the aptly-named and French-governed African island of Réunion, which experts identified "with certainty" as belonging to MH370 thanks to a concealed serial number and a skilled borescope operator; which is to say that there were indeed traces left behind, which had undoubtedly come as a relief to Kingsford Smith's family (he left behind his second wife, Mary, and his son Charles Jr.—who incidentally went on to marry a Mary himself) just as it was a relief to me to know for sure that the aircraft had gone down; and in fact so great was the relief that when I first learned about the discovery on Réunion, it was as though Alison and Beatrice had indeed pulled a Houdini and reappeared before my very eyes, they'd managed to escape oblivion and come back to me as though they'd flown home on that broken piece of wing, a flaperon they called it, because a question, at least one of the hurricane of questions raging inside me, had been answered, for the machine had, without a doubt now, gone down somewhere in the Indian Ocean, broken apart, and the debris had been carried a vast distance via the Indian Ocean Gyre, along with the mountains of trash and plastic particles that form the Indian Ocean Garbage Patch (sister to the Pacific Trash Vortex), to wash up quietly on the rocky shore at Saint-André beach on Réunion, discovered by one Johnny Bègue, head of the island's coastline management group, who was scouring the shoreline for a *kalou*, a stone to use as a pestle for crushing spices—which was like trying to find a needle in a huge pile of needles—when he saw, sticking out of the sand like partially buried treasure, the shredded end of the flaperon, which he and a few colleagues dragged up onto the grass (although it was a tiny section of the Boeing 777's right wing, it was still, relative to a human, very big, practically the size of a coffin) and thus brought to a close a disorienting, stupefying time of uncertainty and anxiety, a time in which I did not know what to think or feel, in which I'd gone numb from a strange and very potent cocktail of despair and hope—there's always been a part of me that believes things will work out for the best—a time in which it seemed as though I was the one who'd disappeared and was, when I did leave the house, eavesdropping on the entire planet. There perhaps has never been a more accurate portrayal of the hackneyed saying that "one man's trash is another man's treasure" than the appearance, the reappearance, of that torn-apart, rusted, completely useless flaperon amid the rocks on that distant sunny island, for it is impossible to describe exactly what that piece of debris, essentially junk, meant to me, the effect it had on me; to say it was worth all the riches on the planet combined doesn't even really come close; to say it became the central point around which my life began to revolve, or from which my life began to spiral outwards, is more accurate; to say that my life was saved by that piece of flotsam is even more accurate again, because I felt as though I was the one floating amid that trash vortex, or not floating but slowly sinking, and just as I was about to take a final breath before disappearing beneath the waves here was something to cling to, useless for every purpose other than keeping me afloat, and with the last ounce of strength I had, I managed to latch onto it and climb aboard; who knows what would have become of me otherwise, I was in a very bad way, unable to eat or sleep, crying more than not crying, suffering a searing headache that lasted almost a year, doing very little work and seeing very few friends, and so I have that man I will never meet, Johnny Bègue, saint, sage, carer for shorelines and grinder of spices, to thank for saving my life, for giving me a life raft—Johnny, if you ever read this, if somehow it manages to find its way to you via the currents of fate: thank you!—for dragging that hunk of metal from the sea like my waterlogged body, because it meant that, when my old friend and true ally Vasily Cosgrove, 'Vazo the Terrible,' came knocking at my door that very same afternoon of the day I first learned of Johnny Bègue and his miraculous discovery, came knocking with the intent of dragging me back to work, with a full list of dates I would have to perform, booked and confirmed, and with the news that if I did not take part in these shows, if I did not travel with them, the whole enterprise would go under; when Vazo came knocking, I was able, without much resistance, to find my way into the shower, pack a bag and stumble squintingly into the daylight for the first time in what seemed a lifetime. Which is not to say that the discovery of the flaperon marked the end of my suffering—if only!—or of the sleepless nights or the constant supposing that spiralled round in my head without respite—those *what if*s that we're told by our therapists not to think, or if we can't help thinking them then to at least ignore: "Do not engage," they say—and nor did it get us any closer to an explanation regarding what exactly happened that morning, apart from ruling out the supernatural and extraterrestrial; but still, for the first time since MH370 vanished from Malaysian military radar at 02:22 on 8 March 2014, we had definitive proof that, regardless of what caused it, the machine did go down somewhere in the Indian Ocean, it did break apart—one theory has it that the aircraft must have plunged vertically into the sea, which would have kept it intact and explain why no debris was found—it succumbed to the laws of physics, there was no unexplainable disappearance, it crashed, everyone was dead—this is difficult to write, but also cathartic—everyone was dead, there was no conspiracy in this regard, the plane was not hidden somewhere deep in the Cambodian jungle, as some had supposed, nor on Diego Garcia, as others had supposed; it had crashed and everyone was dead, Johnny Bègue's discovery of the flaperon was the next-best thing to finding the bodies, which meant that now, instead of living in purgatory, in that holding pattern of uncertainty, instead of not knowing, or at least holding on to the fact of the lack of evidence, I could at last make the descent into hell, and despite how it sounds there was relief in that. It's bizarre to think that such concrete evidence of the deaths of your loved ones can come as good news, but good news it was, relatively speaking, and as luck would have it—despite everything, I do consider myself lucky—Vazo the Terrible picked just the right moment to come knocking at my door—well, it was more like thumping than knocking—and catch the only ray of sunlight to break through my previously impenetrable gloom, the only moment of lightness in a world of darkness and gravity, and although I didn't skip out the door swinging my bags I was at least able, for the first time in almost a year and a half, to collect myself, turn off my computer, and get back to work. There was little time, or money, for rehearsals; as it happened, my time of doubt, uncertainty and anguish was mirrored by the circus', whose popularity had been declining steadily, from once commanding big audiences and rave reviews to being, in order to make way for larger and more profitable tours and more easily recognisable names, relegated to sports fields and parks on the outskirts of town, squeezed into gaps in calendars, and sometimes bumped off schedules by more contemporary acts, music festivals, science fairs, school fêtes, markets, events and enterprises that assumed much more clout than an ancient and ailing circus, and so we took what we could, often where we could—although I say "we," I had very little to do with this tour owing to my hermitude, and with my father's deteriorating health and increasingly limited capacities it was in fact Vazo the Terrible who stepped up and took command of operations and bookings—which meant (perhaps owing to Vasily's Russian blood) that the circuit would be a gruelling one consisting of dozens of dates in a sort of haphazard loop of the country over eleven months, a schedule I would've never accepted, but I was in no state to complain or offer assistance, all I could do was follow instructions and perform. And so the news of the flaperon, which the authorities identified "with certainty" and without doubt as belonging to MH370, news I learned of not via a phone call, a visit or even an email (nor, for that matter, a text message), but through an alert I'd set up, one that gave me a daily list of any bulletins that mentioned that particular flight, which meant that my days were spent trawling through the list, article after article, looking for new information, anything that would help me piece together the story; I received an alert that pointed me towards the story about Johnny and the Flaperon (indeed a modern retelling of 'Jonah and the Whale'), and while it wasn't quite the news I was searching for, it was *news*, for the first time some tangible evidence, hard facts, metal and serial numbers, irrefutable, not guesses or theories or inferences, and I think it was the appearance of these facts, this metal and those serial numbers, the physicality of them, the reality of them, that helped me get my balance after a dizzy and seasick sixteen months, they gave me a horizon via which I could align myself, even though, or rather because these realities, the metal and serial number, brought with them other realities—namely, the plane did indeed crash and break apart, and everyone onboard had perished. I know it sounds bizarre to say, but it was welcome news, even though "welcome" is not quite the right word; in any case, it got me out of the house, out from in front of my computer, out of my seemingly interminable death scrolls, and back to work as a fire performer in Cripp's Circus, which had been touring Australia (and at one point the world) since 1931—

my father, Arthur Keith Cripp, was a WWII orphan who'd been sent to the circus at the age of seven, in 1949, and had become successful at sleight of hand and wrangling big cats before taking over the enterprise when his adoptive parents retired in 1966, whereafter he married the clairvoyant Marigold Hobsbawm and continued touring the country eleven months of every year as owner and proprietor—but was now on the brink of collapse, as it had been at the advent of television (an event that sent my father's adoptive parents into retirement but only made him more focused on success), the only difference being that now my father was no longer as capable of reinventing the show as he had been then—back then, he'd made the acts more and more daring, more death-defying, figuring as he did that the difference between Cripp's Circus and the TV was the proximity of death, for the closer we come to death, the more thrilling the spectacle (this was also, I would later learn, a principle that Harry Houdini held close to his heart: the best thing to get bums on seats is the whiff of death): "We need to give them something they can't get on the damn television!" my father was fond of saying. It was up to me to do what he'd done once before, only now we had much more than TV with which to contend, facing as we did an invasion of innumerable television-like enterprises vying for the same timeslot—and if it wasn't for the diminutive but mighty Vazo, the whole thing would've collapsed completely in my absence—but I was in no fit state to reinvent or reimagine or revivify anything much, yet I knew, in my fog I could still see this clearly, that something needed to be done to keep it going, to keep it all alive, if for no other reason than it was the only thing I had left, for I was becoming the orphan my father once was, my existence, the Earth, the æther was coming back around again, fate was performing its own Immelmann turn, and here I was with no family apart from my slowly vanishing father, while the only home I'd known since my birth was likewise disappearing before my very eyes, and so the least I could do, day after day, night after night, for the next eleven months, was march out into that ring with a smile upon my face and, looking to all the world as though I was in total command of all around and inside me, set myself on fire. And, to be honest, those moments in the ring were a real sanctuary, for self-immolation requires complete concentration and focus as well as solid preparation—these days I wear two layers of wet heat shield material, one layer made of polybenzimidazole (also wet), a fire-retardant suit (for some reason they are always flesh-coloured and make me look like a mummy), on top of which I have my silver reflective firesuit, the costume that the audience sees, which has been covered completely with fire block gel (along with my face and hair) before I'm doused in kerosene, set alight, and on I go; the trick is to keep moving forward so that the fire remains behind you, otherwise you risk very quickly becoming overwhelmed and asphyxiated—fire is a great oxygen thief—even if it's just a slow walk, it's imperative to keep the air flowing, which is the first of two rules to bear in mind, the other being to remember always that fire burns upwards—ie. make sure you are where the flames aren't; simple self-preservation, really—and once I'm on fire and moving into the ring, it isn't simply a matter of wandering around and waving to the crowd before heading offstage again, nothing so simple, for there's a show to put on, it's what we're here for, it's what the audience wants to see—my father always said that you have to build on what's already happening, always ask what else could be included, there's always an opportunity to create a sense of wonder!—and so while I move about the ring I am also juggling fire, spinning fire, twirling fire, swallowing and spitting and breathing fire, like the sun and its solar flares, like the burning bush, flames growling in my ears, the gasping crowd, the feeling that I am creating those feelings of awe and wonder, a feeling that, rather than diminish through repetition over the years, has only become stronger because of the fact, and it is a fact, that awe and wonder have become increasingly rare, or we are now so advanced that everything creates these feelings and we're immune to them—even a simple love-heart text you send to someone sitting right next to you goes up into space first!—despite everything I'm not so jaded as to deny how full of wonder our world is, or should be—it is awe and wonder that I trade in, or did, it is all I have ever known, having been born into a circusing family, my entire purpose has always been to inspire those feelings in others, it was bred into me by my father and mother, great purveyors of wonder themselves, the tingle of pure joy, and not just for children but for everyone, everyone is capable of feeling it, of being there, transported, and thanks to Vazo the Terrible, who stood on the upper rungs of a ladder to douse me in kerro before I went out, that's what I did; with flames pouring off me I shot wonder into people's hearts while carrying inside of me the frozen egg of grief. It was an unlikely venue to start the tour, but from Melbourne we travelled west, bypassing Adelaide and out across the Nullarbor—a journey my grandparents had made when that great highway was a dirt track—into Western Australia and a town called Coolgardie and not, as Vasily had thought, Kalgoorlie, a far larger town than Coolgardie and a far more appropriate place to set up a circus than a former goldmining town now considered a ghost town despite its population of around 850, most of whom, thanks to the gold having dried up early last century, now survived on tourism, an industry that had sprung up in more recent decades as large numbers of people developed a taste for visiting former goldmines and exploring the ruins, which included museums and old hotels, former magistrates' courts and banks and exhibitions of antiquated objects used in the daily lives of pioneers and prospectors—owing to Vasily's geographical error, I managed to see all Coolgardie had to offer while we tried to co-ordinate a quick move to nearby, and far more populous, Kalgoorlie—but, after months crisscrossing the country's barren inland, what became clear to me was that what was most valuable to the tourist trade was not the seen but the unseen, what *wasn't* there as opposed to what *was*—an old pub in the middle of nowhere, of which only the entranceway remained standing, a lone chimney, exposed foundations, a pile of tin sheeting, fading echoes of an ancient world, or as ancient as colonised Australia could get—these were the places that carried the most gravitas, where you had to wait for an opportunity to take a photograph, where you had to bide your time to be alone with nothingness, to be surrounded by almost unlimited empty space, the awesome sprawl of inland Australia, and then be confronted with sudden nothingness, the oblivion of what was, that was the goal, that was what got tourists excited, got me excited (though excited is not the right word), experiences for which I had my dear friend, the troublemaker Vazo the Terrible, to thank, for not only did he get his outback towns mixed up, but the day after our first perform-ance in Coolgardie—to which, it must be said, most of the town turned up, leaving us with the prospect of empty seats for the next two weeks—I woke in my caravan to his incessant fist pummel-ling the door and his booming voice telling me we had places to be, or rather *he* had places to be but I needed to do the driving, and although he managed to coax me outside with the idea that we had to get to Kalgoorlie ASAP in order to find a park or oval to which we might relocate, we did not head for Kalgoorlie, at least not straightaway; instead, holding a map to the dashboard, he directed me around the town and its outskirts, something I was, at first, completely uninterested in, I had little or no energy, my body felt as if it had turned to wet sand, and I often felt like crying, and did, tears coming to my eyes seemingly without any direct inspira-tion, and so roaming aimlessly about an all-but-abandoned mining town in outback Australia was the last thing I wanted to be doing—

exactly what I did want to be doing was not clear to me, all I knew was that it wasn't this—and so we saw the open air exhibition featuring carts, statues and plaques, I barely read any of it, I *couldn't* read any of it, I stared at the words but it was as though my mind couldn't make any sense of them, couldn't articulate the right sounds, or if it did it couldn't ascribe meaning to those sounds, they were just shapes that failed to match up with any knowledge inside me, it was as though there was an invisible and impenetrable force-field around me through which not even knowledge could pass, as though the entire world had been switched off and I was looking at it confused and unsure of what I was seeing, existence had become completely foreign to me and I wasn't sure I hadn't suffered, or was in the process of suffering, some sort of brain damage. Vazo then directed me, in our silver four-wheel-drive that had now turned red on account of the all-swallowing dust, beyond the outskirts of town to the sites of several abandoned goldmines, which were quite frightening when you thought about it, for they consisted of little more than barely man-sized tunnels boring into the earth, into the sides of hills mostly, like black doorways, throats without mouths forged by some sort of metal serpent, through which prospectors walked hunched like servants, shuffling deep into the belly of the landscape; Vasily marvelled at the fact that there weren't more little people known for mining prowess, for they were the perfect size and could undoubtedly have gotten further into the earth, some-thing he proved at a place once known as the Prince of Wales Mine some fifty kilometres west of Coolgardie, where he tugged at the dry-though-rotten boards covering one particular shaft dug into the side of a rocky hill, which came away without huge effort, in fact they practically turned to dust in his hands, everything out here was dust, dust was the almighty ruler, got in everywhere—for weeks afterwards I was beating it out of my clothes and washing it out of my ears—the phrase "from dust to dust" was never truer or more plain to see than it was at the Prince of Wales Mine, everything red and brittle, even the opening of the mineshaft, which should have been a deep oblivion black, was coated in red dust swirling in the sunlight as though the ghost or spirit of the desert floated sentinel over what lay beyond, which is also to say that it hung like a veil, one that Vasily punched a hole through as, having produced from his backpack a flashlight (actually two, one of which he tossed to me), he walked straight in without having to hunch at all, and then he turned to me, his face now taking on the ochre hue of the landscape, and instructed me to follow. He was right; it was bizarre that more people like him were not acknowledged as excellent miners, or even employed as such, for Vazo the Terrible looked as though he could have sprinted off into the darkness and it wouldn't have surprised me if he'd returned with his pockets filled with gold—perhaps this was down to the prejudices and superstitions of the time that were aimed at minorities, in fact undoubtedly it was, an attitude evident in the old expression: "Beware the maimed and impaired!"—an odd saying, when you think about it, because we are all maimed and impaired, none of us function as we feel we should, we've all had bits and pieces run through us and dug out of us and blown off of us; needless to say, I did not wish to follow him inward, I had no interest in exploring an abandoned mineshaft which obviously bore no gold (hence its abandonment) and contained only dust and bats and who knew what else, not to mention the fact that it would not be so easy for me to inch along a tunnel that could barely accommodate my shoulders (men were much smaller in the late nineteenth century) and certainly not my head, I had to stoop sharply, all of which was compounded by the apparent pointlessness of the exploration, one that was confirmed when I called out to a vanishing Vasily, "Why on earth are we doing this?" and he replied, "Why not, you frightened little girl!" and his voice boomed in my ears and reverberated all around me as I pushed my head resignedly forward into that dusty black hole. Perhaps my little companion had become temporarily infected with the spirit of exploration that whispered in the trees and tussock out there on the fringes of the Australian desert, for he was indeed not the first person of European descent to say, "Why not, you frightened little girl!" before marching off into the great unknown, far from it; the place practically creaked with their bones, and so his polyrhythmic voice, multiplied exponentially by that tunnel, could have been all the voices of all the outback explorers, famous, infamous and forgotten, who'd come before him, laden with the gravity of endeavour, a motivation to which I was, at that juncture, entirely immune; nevertheless, what else could I do but follow his lead, and besides, the outside air was completely mad with heat and hotter even than the night before when I'd been engulfed in flames, and so I twisted my flashlight to life and entered the coolness and darkness which, once I got going, seemed blessed with its own gravity and drew me in almost without any effort on my part, and thus I sallied forth into those black reaches brushed, despite my defences, by the wing of exploration on which hordes of prospectors had flocked to these parts in the late nineteenth century in search of the King of Metals, few more renowned than a certain David Wynford Carnegie, a dapper, striking Englishman, born in London to James Carnegie, 9th Earl of Southesk, who after dropping out of college in 1892 and heading for Ceylon at age twenty-two to work on a tea plantation, found himself nearly dead of boredom after only two weeks and thus, accompanied by his dear friend, Lord Percy Douglas, older brother of Oscar Wilde's Lord Alfred, set off for Albany, Western Australia, where in the month of September they steamed into the glimmering King George's Sound with visions of intrepid explorations and the vast fortunes that supposedly awaited in what Carnegie referred to in his book about his Australian life, *Spinifex and Sand*, as "that newly-discovered land of Ophir."

Indeed newly-discovered it was, for on 17 September 1892 the prospector Arthur Wellesley Bayley had received a reward lease of twenty acres after discovering some five hundred-odd ounces of gold at a place they called Fly Flat (anyone who has visited in the summer will know how the place got its name, which was another reason why my entering the cool, black mine-shaft was such a relief), a discovery

David Wynford Carnegie

that precipitated a mad rush, arguably the biggest in the nation's history, out to the area that was quickly renamed Coolgardie by the warden, Finnerty, and summarily opened (again by Finnerty) on 20 September—astounding how quickly bureaucracies can function when there are riches to be had!—and thus, not even off the boat, the two English gentlemen were caught up in the buzz that swept through the port at King George's Sound and north to Perth, out to Southern Cross and further east to Fly Flat, aka Coolgardie. Despite their pedigree, the pair was rather short of money on arrival and were, especially after getting word of the find at Fly Flat, keen to try their collective hand at prospecting, for not only were there riches to be had in the "land of Ophir," but this adventure was far more exciting than picking tea on a plantation in Ceylon, which although exotic and distant was also completely *known*; the even-more-distant brown land that now spread out before them was perfect for a handsome, idle college dropout and his misfit (soon-to-be) Marquess midshipman mate to make their names, because this was *terra nullius*, the next-best thing to exploring on the moon, which is to say completely unknown; as they stepped off the steamer at King George's Sound they were leaving behind what they knew of the world and themselves, leaving the gravity, the touchstone, of their rational, civilised, everyday lives onboard the ship and marching forth on their first real adventure, college boyishness still in their veins, into a world where what kept your feet on the ground was different to back home—different even to colonial Ceylon—in short, a world they did not understand, the Antipodes, one which, so they were led to believe, rewarded the spirit of adventure and discovery, which is practically all the two boys had brought with them. And so from King George's Sound in Albany they set out for Perth, then from Perth to Southern Cross and from there on to Coolgardie riding the wave of diggers now migrating east, a journey that would give them a taste of prospecting before they'd even reached the plump goldfields, for such was the blinding heat of the sun and the dryness of the earth, that water became even more precious than gold, the landscape playing tricks with its rippled air that had them saying to themselves (often there was no strength left to say it to anyone else), "Just a little further," which was the digger spirit, "Keep pushing"; what horrors they must have seen even before they reached Bayley's Reward, men and horses mad with thirst dragging themselves another mile along the increasingly beaten track, fighting each other selfishly for just a mouthful of water held over at the base of granite outcrops along the way, like little beacons of hope these hills appeared in stages between Southern Cross and Coolgardie, and if it were not for them (and, it must be said, the camels) the track could not have remained open; what the two English gentlemen hadn't counted on was arriving in one of the hottest parts of the planet in the middle of a drought, or as Carnegie called it "a water-famine," with heat so intense you had to cool your mining tools in the shade or risk burning your hands, which meant they'd arrived at the newly named Coolgardie at the worst possible time, not only after gold had already been discovered but in the middle of a dry spell, one so severe that those in the field had to rely on horse-drawn teams that carted water tanks into the township once a day from a distant supply, which were often quickly depleted and expensive, and very soon the authorities put up notices stating that the track out to Coolgardie would soon be closed. Carnegie would find little gold over the next few years, despite canvassing the interior accompanied by the auspiciously named Frenchman, Augustus 'Gus' Luck; and it was not as a prospector that he would be remembered—and he *would* be remembered, much to his satisfaction—but as an explorer, for after tiring of searching for gold for others he proposed his grandest scheme yet: to traverse an uncharted and unknown passage between Coolgardie and Halls Creek, some 1,600 kilometres as the crow flies, comprised of little but the hellish country of the Gibson and Great Sandy deserts, armadas of flies and, of course, the searing furnace of the sun, as relentless as Carnegie's ambition, an ambition that saw him depart Coolgardie on 9 July 1896 with a crew of four (bushman Joe Breaden and his Indigenous "companion" Warri, and the prospectors Godfrey Massie and Charles Stansmore)

JOSEPH A. BREADEN. HON. DAVID W. CARNEGIE. WARRI. GODFREY E. MASSIE.
MEMBERS OF THE CARNEGIE EXPLORING EXPEDITION.

north to Menzies and onward into the grip of the desert, which indeed took a firm hold of the group, for within a month they were suffering terribly from a lack of water—some of the party were by now experiencing the painful cramps and vomiting brought on by severe dehydration—and Carnegie was compelled to deploy his tactic of seeking out and capturing a native man (a "King Billy" or "buck," as he referred to them) and forcing him to reveal the source of his water, which on this particular occasion, with the party in dire need, involved giving chase to a young black man whom they'd found digging in the sand in search of an iguana—he'd been so focused on capturing his meal he hadn't noticed the sickly band of explorers eyeing him off—and who'd tried in vain to run away but was soon leashed to Carnegie's belt and commanded via the usual fumblings with the native language and a crude series of gestures to take them to water, which he would do eventually, though not before taking them on a five-hour trek through the inferno to a "waterhole" that was nothing but a bowl of dry, cracked clay—no doubt an act of devilishness on the part of their captive, whom Carnegie, at least in his memoir, praised for his cunning and claimed to understand why, in the middle of the Australian desert, he would not wish to show a party of five thirsty men as well as their horses and camels to his tribe's only supply of water, which would have been drunk in an instant—it would have been funny if it weren't for the seriousness of the situation, for they were all of them out on their feet *before* they started this five-hour detour through the insane heat and dust—perhaps their captive thought he could, like the ever-retreating Russians had done to Napoleon's army almost a century before on the opposite side of the planet and in conditions that were the extreme opposite, let the climate bring down the enemy; perhaps if he could lead them deeper into that land of scorched earth, the sun would do his work for him, the landscape would provide. But it was not to be, for they would not let him go, and seemingly he too was beginning to suffer a lack of hydration, no thanks to the salted meats Carnegie fed him, an act that was, according to the explorer, intended to promote friendship and good-will between them—despite Carnegie's act of captivity—as well as to promote a thirst in the young man, a double-pronged ploy that proved successful, for after the dustbowl he'd led them to, he took them to an underground spring on the fringes of the Gibson Desert, a spring so well-camouflaged that the party would have had zero chance of finding it without their prisoner, for it presented itself merely as three depressions in the rocky surface of the valley, depressions that turned out to be tunnels each large enough to accommodate a man, and so, via a rope they lowered themselves into one of them, Carnegie descended into the darkness, blind from the sudden lack of light but also soothed by the sudden absence of sun and heat, a relief so unfamiliar he'd almost forgotten it, until his boots touched the soft sand almost ten metres below—in fact he did not so much touch the sand as sink into it up to his shins, whereon he started to dig in the hope of finding a soak as he'd done so many times before, digging excitedly, ecstatically, and using up far more energy than he had in reserve; but as luck would, or rather wouldn't, have it, no water was forthcoming, the sand re-mained coarse and dry, and the leader of the expedition, down in the black belly of the landscape, started to curse the young buck who seemed intent on leading them all to certain death, and if it wasn't for the light of the candle, which he now ignited—a different sort of "match test"—his fury might have gotten the better of him, for as the warm yellow light emanated onto the rock walls it be-came clear that he'd landed in some sort of cave or chamber, and not only that, but from this cave there ran two passages, one west and up, the other east and further down into the earth; all of a sudden he forgot about the cunning native and headed off east with renewed hope, first having to slouch then to drop to his hands and knees as the jagged ceiling and walls tapered to such a size as to allow only a crawl—the original Australian crawl—and although the tunnel was already sloping downwards it now grew even steeper and it was all Carnegie could do to stop himself skidding and slipping and sliding against the sharp rock, sliding to God knows where, to oblivion, down into the centre of the earth—his eyes in the candlelight must have been all white—until he came to a stop and saw, just below him, the reflection of his candle in the darkness, and reaching out for it he touched the surface of the gleaming black pool as though he was afraid it might run away in fright or evaporate beneath his fingers, never had anything been so miraculous, never had anything hinted at the presence of the Almighty—he cried out "Thank God! Thank God!" even though he was not at all religious—not even the King of Metals could ever hope to shine with such lustre or be of such incredible value, for it not only saved the lives of Carnegie and his team, but it also enabled them to continue their journey into the unknown towards Halls Creek, which they now made in reasonable time and almost without incident—save for a single tragedy in which one of the party, Charlie Stansmore, with Halls Creek only ten or so miles away, slipped while carrying his gun, setting off a charge that blasted right through his heart and killed him instantly, a calamity that sent a shock through the whole gang, one that David Wynford Carnegie, ever the optimist, interpreted as preferable: "better so than a lingering death in the desert, a swift and sudden call instead of perhaps slow tortures of thirst and starvation!"—a sentiment I couldn't agree with more, much better the lights are shut off instantly than to endure their gradual dimming; in the time of my self-imposed house arrest, those days and months following the disappearance of MH370, when I went out only for groceries and the occasional ray of sunlight, when my every waking hour was spent scouring news websites and conspiracy theory blogs, days of wishing for my own death, when everything hurt and yet nothing hurt, when my research took me into the exceedingly dark corners of the internet, into which I waded like a sleepwalker, describing in cold detail the medical facts about what happens to a person when they are killed in an air crash—for this was the reality I was faced with, and if there was no hope of finding the aircraft in which Alison and Beatrice had lost their lives, then at least I could hope to understand how they had died and, hopefully, assure myself that their suffering, like poor old Charlie Stansmore, wasn't protracted; it made for gruelling reading, I've often regretted having explored it in the first place—in hindsight, I suspect my compulsion to face these facts had more to do with making myself suffer, a kind of self-flagellation, for the shame I'd felt in surviving, for carrying on while they could not, and the simultaneous wish, one that has come and gone like a ghost from a dim room, for my life to end—and yet I did take a sort of comfort in it because while the location of their bodies remained a mystery, what had happened to them was less so—not that I could take anything as fact, but there were things I could reasonably assume—and at least that was something; for instance, it is generally accepted that air crash deaths are very quick, practically instantaneous, such are the extreme forces involved, which are somewhere in the vicinity of 50–200G, and that means, obviously, that there is minimal suffering, so while one post-mortem examination report from twenty-eight of the hundred and eighteen people who perished aboard British European Airways Flight 548 on 18 June 1972 lists the various causes of death as "fractured skull, fractured cervical spine, ruptured aorta, ruptured liver and ruptured heart," the examiner also notes that the victims "had received injuries which would lead to immediate loss of consciousness or death" (an interesting sidenote is that the bodies are often found in groups defined by class—ie. first-class and economy—and size—ie. the children are usually in one place and full-grown adults in another; physics, apparently); indeed, an investigator into an Air France disaster concluded that "the death was very fast... and the physical pains caused by multiple traumas were probably felt but very briefly, the time of 'useful consciousness' being very short," all of which was a horrific kind of comfort; but as I said, nothing was a given, and so while I tried to cling to the likely swiftness of this sort of death, there were other eventualities, some acceptable and some dreadful, that had to be considered; why did I look here? I don't know; I wanted to expose myself to what Alison and Beatrice had experienced, to their pain, their fate; madness; crushing; but to be honest it was something my mind returned to over and again and so, I thought, if I could peer into the very depths of my own horror then maybe these questions would grow silent, if I could dive as deep as I could go, if I could butt my head against the seabed of grief and find the limits of my own emotional endurance, then I could say for sure that it could not get any worse, and so I tried to flay myself into healing by becoming intimate with reports of the various forces to which the human body is subjected in the unlikely event of an emergency, reports I read over and over again, phenomena I ingested like breakfast in the hope that, like the miracle of flight itself, all of it might become banal and therefore impotent; and so, from memory alone, without consulting another text other than the black river of facts and data that now flows right through me, I here list them:

- If the crash is slow and you have time to say to yourself "We're crashing," or if the pilot comes over the PA and says "Brace for impact!", your body will do its best to try to protect you with what are commonly called fight or flight responses, which become manifest when your adrenal glands secrete adrenaline and norepinephrine into your bloodstream and cause your heart rate to escalate, your breathing to become more efficient and your lungs to expand, a process that also boosts your pain threshold and renders your muscles more responsive; if you could run or fight, your body is now as primed as it will ever be, but because you are in an aircraft, and thus cannot go anywhere or do anything about the situation, other than the subtle numbing sensations brought on by the adrenaline, your natural response to such an unnatural situation is practically useless; what's worse is that it also causes the brain to become hyperalert, which sounds like a good thing, but activating what's called "memory packing" means that everything slows down, or at least that's how it seems to you because in this state of awareness your mind is absorbing every detail and filing it away in case it's useful in helping you get out of the situation, and because there's more to absorb it simply takes longer, which makes every moment seem extended, which again is extremely useful if you need to react quickly but at thirty thousand feet is essentially torture; which is to say that these processes that are there to protect us may in fact cause added suffering.

- The silver lining to the above is that there's a strong likelihood you won't know that you're crashing until the last second, especially in cases of explosions or serious mechanical failures where the machine makes a sudden and drastic change of direction; also, in many instances, the pilots will be too busy trying not to crash to say anything over the PA; either that or they won't want to cause a stir.

- A sudden loss of cabin pressure, following an explosion or mechanical failure, would be the preferable scenario (given the choice), for the forces during what's known as explosive decompression are such that you lose consciousness immediately before your body, perhaps a split second later, is completely disassembled—ie. torn apart.

- Also tearing you apart will be your seatbelt, which stops you bumping about during turbulence and helps restrain children and intoxicated passengers, but at terminal velocity, when the aircraft, all three hundred tonnes of it, plunges into the earth, it becomes lethal, holding your body *in situ* from the waist down while the torso, head and arms continue at the same velocity as the plane; a force that, needless to say, our bodies are not designed to withstand.

- If you hit the earth (or ocean) at great speed, chances are you're already unconscious due to the aforementioned explosive decompression or the incredible G-forces which occur during a sudden change of direction, such as when the pilot executes a sharp bank or the aircraft goes into a spiral and/or a very deep dive, in which case, under the extreme load, you will initially lose spatial awareness, then you will lose your eyesight and any understanding of the situation before slipping into unconsciousness. For me, after all my research, this is the absolute best way to go; there will undoubtedly be a moment of terror—and hopefully your adrenal glands will flood you with their numbing concoction—followed by pure oblivion and blankness. Together with asphyxiation, which follows a similar pattern leading to unconsciousness, it is this scenario that is the most humane and, while far from gentle, involves the least amount of suffering.

- The forces involved in getting you to the ground will do all of the above to you, but if you have come through this phase more or less intact, or at least still alive, the situation becomes exceedingly more perilous, for the impact will, like sudden decompression, tear you limb from limb, or if it doesn't quite do that it will probably cause your internal organs to liquify as they try to leave your body and become crushed and smeared against your skeletal system and skin; to wit: your lungs will puncture, as will your bowels, which alone are enough to fill the rest of your body with bile and blood, while other liquids fill the spaces around your heart, lungs and stomach. Imagine what's being done to the aircraft inside and out; it's exactly what's happening to you too.

- There will likely be fire to contend with, for aviation fuel combined with shredded metal and searing hot engines is probably going to combust; and it won't be just any old fire because this sort of fuel burns at around 815ºC and will engulf the aircraft much faster than you can run, even in an uninjured state and without the obstacles and mess around you. (I am almost certain this would not have happened to Alison and Beatrice because the data tells us that the aircraft continued moving and responding for something in the order of seven-and-a-half or eight-and-a-half hours, and it is the opinion of the authorities that when it did go down it was due to a lack of fuel, which means there would have been no fire to speak of. Still, it is worth noting, for after a lifetime of setting myself on fire I am well aware of the unpredictable and deadly nature of flames—I have the scars to prove it, on my hands, back and face—which can appear at any time and change course at any time without warning and often seemingly without reason. If you have closely observed a fire, a big fire, you will know what I mean when I say that it is a complex and wily organism.) So, even with the dramatically reduced likelihood of fire, when the aircraft had reached the outer limit of its window and was probably over water when it came down, you can never say that the chance of fire is definitively zero.

- On the other hand, if the aircraft ditches into water, all of the above applies except for fire, but in this scenario you can swap fire for hypothermia, which occurs when the body's temperature falls below 35°C; in cold sea waters at night, this can happen within minutes and will result in the complete shutdown of your organs as they begin to fail one after the other, a process that actually sounds a lot worse than, apparently, it feels, for other than the initial fear and stress the gradual shutting down of your body feels a lot like going to sleep.

- Seating, as in the seats themselves, also presents an issue, since the seats can concertina under heavy impact, trapping and crushing passengers as the tail of the aircraft tries to make its way forward to the cockpit, effectively creating a huge, multi-fanged metallic jaw; alternatively, while still in the air, a sudden and large enough fissure in the bodywork can suck you out under depressurisation—complete with seating—scattering you to the winds, in which case you'll be rendered unconscious from the G-forces and/or decompression, and if you're not dead already the impact with the ground/water will finish you off. Possibly the worst way to go, strapped in and conscious all the way down. Unlikely, but possible. I dread to think.

- Lastly, there is the extended accident unfolding over many minutes or even hours, which in the past has led to passengers having the time and wherewithal to digest what is happening, and likely to happen, and even to compose letters to loved ones, poems and journal-like passages that detail their thoughts on all manner of topics from happiness to meaning and regret; and while this is not a hugely common scenario, it is common enough to warrant a mention, for no doubt we've all heard stories of this sort of thing occurring, letters of love, kindness, forgiveness and tenderness being scratched out on whatever is to hand as disaster unfolds all around—just think, in those final moments, be they minutes or hours, in this age of information and instantaneous communication, reaching for the tried and trusted pen and paper, harking back to the days of the *Argus* when reporters jotted furiously in real time; an incredible act of hope, really, in a completely hopeless situation—it makes one feel that, at heart, we are, at least the vast majority of us, optimists, for what chance really has a handwritten note aboard a disintegrating aircraft thirty thousand feet in the sky have of finding its way into the hands of its addressee? practically zero because how will it *not* be burned, soaked, torn apart, lost or simply picked up by some big machine that collects the debris of air disasters and hauls it all off to a refuse station or examination hangar?—and yet it happens, on the brink of catastrophe; with enough time for passengers to acknowledge what's happening to them and what's likely to happen to them in the near future, they scramble about for pen and paper and commit their deepest feelings and thoughts to the page; a testament to impossible hope that reveals to us something about writing itself, the act of writing, of getting things down, and that is this: it is a form of communication that refuses to acknowledge the boundary between the living and the dead, or even the difference between them, which means that by writing you are speaking directly into the hearts of your intended, living or dead, near or far, and the text works like a bridge or a caterpillar track, the sort used by military tanks and heavy machinery, via which you can make the impossible journey, reach out across tyrannical distances, time, dimensions, issuing a call that is not subject to the laws of physics and soundwaves and reverberations and oscillations, a silent call whose potency derives from its very soundlessness; what's more, we know this instinctively, for why else would so many people, *in the middle of an air crash*, think to lay out their thoughts and feelings, think to commune with their loved ones via writing, by penning a letter that stands no chance at all of being sent or received, that would take an absolute miracle, a flat-out marvel, to get the words into the hands of the subject?, and yet it is not that uncommon in the midst of tragedy for the writing to commence, for the letters to go out, while everything is on fire, to go out, to go down amid the flames, for the bridge of words to extend between loved ones, in an endeavour to draw them near and hold them and feel the intensity, the heat, of their presence.

Deep inside the old Prince of Wales mine, with Vazo the Terrible's whistling (for some reason it was *La Marseillaise*) filling up the darkness, the tunnel descended rapidly and I found I had to steady myself with my free hand against the by turns jagged and smoothly cut walls as well as keep my head down because the ceiling height was unpredictable and potentially lethal, if anything it was growing lower by the inch as the air grew cooler and once or twice we had to, both of us, duck just as a bat started flapping about in the narrow confines causing me to jump and I caught my scalp on a ridge of rock which immediately brought tears to my eyes. "Careful, mate," said Vasily without turning around, and in a rush of anger brought on by the sudden pain I asked him what we were doing down here, because I for one did not wish to be here, in the middle of nowhere on the outskirts of a town that was barely alive, where nothing at all had happened since the days of the gold rush, and for that matter where we were not even supposed to be—we should have been in Kalgoorlie, for God's sake, not down a mine on the fringes of the desert!—"We're almost there," said my companion, finally turning to me with an excited expression that caught the white light of my torch; perhaps it was the shadows, or perhaps it was just his enthusiasm, or even the narrowing tunnel, but Vasily suddenly seemed larger, more commanding, which was why he was so good in the ring, incidentally, for despite his diminished stature he was able to project something of a dominating presence and hold the audience in the palm of his little hand—it was Vasily who roamed round the ring before my performances, geeing up the crowd, getting them on the edges of their seats or even on their feet before meeting me offstage with an encouraging word, a splash of kerro and flick of a flame—and it was this attitude, this *air* he possessed, that kept me moving in his wake, not only further into this tunnel but also further into that tour that quite possibly saved my life. Soon the mine opened once more and I was able to stand completely upright (could have even jumped a little if I'd had a mind to) and we now made our way with ease in the cooling air until we came to a fork at which, with a moment's hesitation as though he was trying to recall directions, Vasily indicated that we should go left then, coming as we did to a dead end, he led us back to now take the right turning, which within about thirty metres opened and revealed, even with our torches going, a pale blue light up ahead, one that intensified as we drew nearer to such a degree that I found I could shut mine off and still see the way perfectly well; Vazo too pocketed his torch as the tunnel opened into a massive chamber that was lit from the ground at five points, the blue security lights shining up the rock walls and over what looked to be heavy duty scaffolding all the way along one side of the chamber; this wall was separated from its opposite by about a hundred metres, easily the size of a football field, and squinting into the brightness I could make out yet more scaffolding down there and a large, black archway opening up in another direction, which Vazo pointed to and said, "That's how they get all the heavier machinery in," machinery that was clearly required to build the structures towering above us, for it could not have been done by hand, that's for sure, and so, according to Vasily, they'd bored out one of the two existing tunnels in order to facilitate the construction of these scaffolds, which turned out to not be scaffolds at all (or at least the majority weren't) but racking that would soon accommodate underground servers and data storage units. It was still in the early phases of construction and supposedly (though who's to say?) the first of its kind in the country; there were already several notable underground facilities in other parts of the world—ie. Iron Mountain in the United States, Swiss Fort Knox in Switzerland, The Bunkers in the UK and Bahnhof Pionen in Sweden—many of which made use of abandoned military bunkers, with the exception of Iron Mountain which was built inside an old iron mine and comprised a 1.7 million-square-foot campus some sixty-five metres underground, an enterprise that began stealthily in 1951 and had grown to become one of the most renowned data storage facilities in the world—it was, for instance, where Bill Gates stored his Corbis photographs, a refrigerated, hermetically sealed collection of over one hundred million images and eight hundred thousand videos that form a visual history of the twentieth century; it was also where many of the original Frank Sinatra master recordings were held, as well as countless masters for countless artists owned by entertainment giants like Sony, Warner and Universal, plus the original wills of Charles Dickens, Charles Darwin and Princess Diana and almost two thousand unclaimed, presumably "lost" cans of nitrate film that made up the Iron Mountain Collection at the Academy Film Archive—"the Mountain" was known as the largest privately owned underground storage facility in the world and was possibly (though we could never say for sure because of the sensitive nature of the data storage enterprise) the first of its kind anywhere; however, as its reputation grew, other companies began seeking out their own underground opportunities, and by the time Vasily and I entered the former Prince of Wales mine outside Coolgardie, many of them were starting to realise the wealth of already-excavated *terra nullius* beneath the West Australian deserts. Of course, conducting the requisite earthworks themselves would have been far too expensive, prohibitively so, but because the mines were already there, these companies could buy the land cheaply and fit out the subterranean tunnels and chambers for the purpose of storing vast amounts of information in their underground clouds; moreover, so Vasily told me as we walked around the half-constructed facility—he'd been told, so he said, by the manager of the Goldfields Exhibition Museum in Coolgardie the day before, an excitable German, I was to discover, whose name was Otto and who, via his engaging accent, wished to walk you through the town's history in what felt like real time—there was the ever-reliable Outback sun, the energy from which was to be harvested and used to power, cool, ventilate, dehumidify and protect the site via solar panel farms, meaning that the data storage companies didn't need to hook up to the grid and would remain self-sufficient and sustainable both economically and environmentally; it was all there just waiting for them. Walking around in the harshness of the powerful halogen lights—in a few more weeks, Vasily said, we would not be able to enter so easily, for it was getting to the stage where they'd have to set up security; they'd only waited this long because no-one ever came out here, which was another advantage of the location: the almost complete absence of people—but for now we moved about freely, and in the metallic-diesel air, vastly different from the wet-rock smell back in the narrow tunnel, I envisaged the future of this place, of the whole country for that matter, a nation founded on natural resources, not invention or ingenuity, but on what could be dug up by those diggers, on holes bored into the earth, minerals extracted and shipped off—how much of Australia is now in other parts of the world? how many of the world's rich and famous wear markers of their status retrieved from the Australian dirt?—and this mining endeavour not only unearthed valuable resources but also, unwittingly, created another: empty space; for as the world generated more and more information, day in day out, new pictures, videos, documents, programs, software, social media posts; as more and more of history was being archived, it did not all simply vanish into the æther, did not fade away into the past, it required storing, and storage required space; increasingly it will become the world's most valuable commodity, not for farming or housing or production, but for the storage of information, and the abandoned goldmines will open once again, activity will return to these parts because empty space, negative space, these voids in the landscape, will be worth their weight in gold, maybe even more so, and once again we'll find ourselves sitting on incalculable riches, potentially every record of every occurrence in the history of existence, for that was the way it was going, every detail of every day in the life of everyone, you and me, tucked away down here, every answer to every question, every fact unarguable, the hard evidence incontrovertible, all *knowing* kept under lock and key and twenty-four-hour surveillance in an old mine in the Australian desert; this was just the beginning, this gigantic chamber in the old Prince of Wales mine, fitted out with everything it needed to house subterranean mountains of knowledge, was the tip of the iceberg, as it were, for it will undoubtedly trigger a new wave of interest and activity, not so much a goldrush as a voidrush, a new kind of space race, one that doesn't go up but rather down, into instead of away from, which is to say that those diggers from the old days, the original diggers of the late nineteenth century, the likes of David Wynford Carnegie and Gus Luck and Lord Percy Douglas, were not only getting in while the going was good but also carving out our future, launching us into the age of knowledge, of fact in text, photographs, videos and charts, birthdates and death dates and everything in between, the complete wikipedic history of everything packed into these dusty mines, the landscape murmuring with their ghosts, groaning with the weight of knowledge—which is curious because those men, those great explorers, were insistent about going into the unknown; there was no interest at all in the known; the main objective was to blaze a trail, just as Carn-egie had done between Coolgardie and Halls Creek; the lure was not knowing, so much so that in a letter dated 16 November 1898 to an explorer friend in Australia (by now Carnegie was back in England wondering what to do with himself), one William "Harry" Tietkens, he laments: "now that so many tracks cross each other over the interior... there is no great 'unknown' left [and] I feel that it is wiser to look to some newer country," which incidentally he did, sailing for Africa in December 1899 to take up the position of Assistant Resident of the Middle Niger in Nigeria, a position he held for barely eleven months until, in a moment of what some might call poetic justice, in the early morning of 27 November 1900, while searching the village of Tawari for a fugitive by the name of Gana, he was shot in the thigh with a poison arrow and died not fifteen minutes later at the tender age of twenty-nine, having made some-thing of a name for himself, if not quite a fortune, and sought out the unknown the world over until he stumbled across the Great Unknown in that tiny Nigerian village. And now, over a century later, when there are even fewer great unknowns than in Carnegie's day, data storage companies are making moves to enter the tunnels these men dug in the landscape and to fill them up with knowledge, infinite knowledge, and as Vasily and I surveyed that subterranean construction site, the scents of metal and diesel and industry in the air, I welcomed this development, welcomed it wholeheartedly, because with the wealth of information packed into our soil, mere metres beneath our feet, it was my hope (and remains so) that answers would grow, would grow up through the rock like a persistent vine or soak and break through the burned crust of desert, a sudden burst of life in a lifeless expanse, because someone has to know something, for heaven's sake, with all the monitoring and data processing and satellite information and radio broadcasts and cell towers and phone calls and selfies and texts and uploads and downloads and radar and protocol and Hubble telescopes and tiny borescopes, with everything monitored all the time, somebody must know something about what happened to that aircraft that was carrying my wife and daughter, some instrument must have recorded what happened that night over the Indian Ocean, there must be an overlooked message on somebody's phone, surely in the time before the satellite lost contact with the aircraft someone switched their phone off flight mode to send out an SOS or a final farewell—in fact, a study at the time by the Consumer Electronics Association found that roughly 30% of airline passengers forgot or refused to power down their devices on any given flight, and it was also estimated that around the same time one in five people owned a smartphone, which means that on a flight containing two hundred and twenty-seven passengers (discounting the crew, who we assume knew better), it is likely that 13.62 passengers had their smartphones on, which means that there could have been *at least* 13.62 phones (allowing for other brands) idling away in a bag or pocket searching for a handshake with a mobile tower (handshakes that are entirely trackable), and while there are issues around connectivity over vast bodies of water as well as at high cruising altitudes, it is not unheard of for smartphones to have coverage during a flight, and while the airline has maintained that there was no wifi available to passengers on MH370, first class passengers did have access to seat-mounted air-to-ground telephones from which they could make calls and send emails, and yet there are no records of any communications coming from that quarter either; the only record we do have, and it is one that proves the crew were also susceptible to bending the rules, which raises other questions, is that the co-pilot, twenty-seven-year-old Fariq Abdul Hamid, who had his whole life ahead of him, did indeed leave his phone on and it did indeed achieve a handshake, unfortunately this was while the aircraft was over Penang and was being duly tracked by military satellite, which is to say that Hamid's indiscretion tells us little more than we already knew, only that it was not unheard of for even the crew to be blasé about certain protocols—now, we say it was being "tracked by military satellite," but that is a slightly misleading phrase because it suggests active intent on the part of the military and gives us an image of uniformed, buzz-cut men standing in a dark room watching the radar and looking puzzled as to why MH370 was doing what it was doing; no, this was not the case at all, and it is more accurate to say that the Malaysian military radar *just happened to pick it up* as a consequence of its range and coverage; no-one was watching as the whole catastrophe unfolded, which in an age when you can locate your telephone, laptop, car, anything really in seconds, when there are so many tracking devices all around us bleeping and blipping and shaking hands and making contact, there must be some explanation, some data, something filed away in a phone record or handshake data from, say, a Burmese telecommunications company, there simply has to be something somewhere, a moment, a millisecond, recorded by some system whose primary task was elsewhere but that nevertheless *just happened to pick up*, managed to catch, something in its net, a cache of unsent messages, for instance, or failed social media posts, something that would unravel one of the biggest mysteries in aviation history, more so than the disappearances of Sir Charles Kingsford Smith or Harry Rickards' grandson, Harry Frank 'Jim' Broadbent, or the disappearance of Houdini's Voisin after its performances in Australia, more so than most disappearances, really, aviation or not, something that would make us say, "Ah, well *that* makes sense!" for the chances of such a huge machine, with all the attendant technology and surveillance, with everything we have at our disposal, combined with the fact that the chances of being in a fatal air crash are eleven million to one, and the chances of surviving one are around 95%, frankly it's a miracle anyone dies like this, the numbers make it seem impossible—you could say that it's miraculous it even happened at all; we tend to think of miracles in a positive light, jaw-dropping changes of fortune for the better, reprieves from certain doom, unexplainable, superhuman feats of skill and daring, but in the context of the sheer unlikelihood of a Boeing 777-200ER dropping out of all contact, its disappearance is very much something of a miracle—how could an object so huge slip through the minutest of cracks and vanish without a trace (save for the equally miraculous find of tenacious Réunion beachcomber Johnny Bègue)?—indeed, it is certainly more miraculous and mesmerising (and it is mesmerising, the whole world was transfixed for a time; many still are) than other more predictable disappearances, such as those during the West Australian gold-rush, when you had groups of explorers risking life and limb in an effort to broaden the scope of the known world; a case in point being the Calvert Expedition in Western Australia, which on 13 June 1896 set off as a company of seven men and twenty camels from Mullewa in Western Australia with a mission to explore the vast unknown reaches of the Great Sandy Desert, only to have two of the men—second-in-command Charles Wells and mineralogist and photographer George Jones—vanish after taking a detour from the main party, seemingly swallowed up by the desert; news of which reached our man David Wynford Carnegie, who it turned out had just arrived in Halls Creek having successfully led his expedition from Coolgardie through the desert where they founded and named many sites including the lifesaving subterranean Empress Spring, having only lost one man, poor Charlie Stanmore who'd fumbled his gun, and as sad and unfortunate as that was, Carnegie was still intent on proving himself to the world (not to mention to his app-arently unimpressed father James Carnegie, 9th Earl of Southesk) and certainly up for an adventure, and so, given that he'd just come through the desert parallel to the Calvert Expedition and knew the area and the terrain, he was the likely candidate to head the search and rescue party, but for reasons "that need not be gone into,"

117

according to Carnegie's account, his party was told to hold fire at Halls while a certain William Frederick Rudall was sent in by the state authorities—it appears that the co-ordination of the search was more political than anything else, and from Carnegie's tone one could argue he felt he was in a far better position to find the missing men alive, but there were appearances to keep up as well as people to please; such is the nature of many a search and rescue operation, as we've seen in the Indian Ocean, the likes of which usually turn up nothing. As we might have expected, the mission did indeed turn up nothing, and before Carnegie and his men were asked to step in and head out into the desert, the two missing men were given up for dead, which might have been the end of the matter had the leader of the Calvert Expedition, Larry Wells, cousin to the lost Charles Wells, not continued with the search and at last managed to find their decaying bodies some five months later on the very track that the rest of the party had taken after their separation (at what is now known by the doleful handle Separation Well); and not only did the search party find the bodies but they also found the pair's diaries, which Carnegie paraphrases in his own account of the episode, telling of thirst, sickness and starvation, disorientation, suffering and absolute exhaustion before each man lay down to die "in the scanty shade of a gum tree," though not before, as Carnegie reminds us, writing with "dying fingers," overcome by the inferno, messages for those who would be left to mourn them, scratching out a final farewell, last thoughts, regrets and hopes, hope above all that someone would find their words, or rather hope to feel the presence of their loved ones in the words they were writing, to commune across the plain of life and death, to hold them one last time and try to impart a sense of the love they felt, the love that might redeem the situation, the only thing that could hope to redeem the situation—or perhaps it is only in these situations that such thought, feeling and action is possible, when everything is brought into sharp focus as the deadline draws near—the hope that someone will find what has been written, that in the vast sea of spinifex and sand, someone just might stumble across their remains and deliver to their families a voice from beyond the grave, a voice telling them that everything's okay, wrapping up their lives, bringing them to a close and getting out what needs getting out, what needs saying, perhaps what has not been said before, or has not been said in a very long time, the I love yous, the I'm sorrys, the thank yous, the don't fall aparts, dashed off with dying fingers using the last vestiges of awareness and composure, the last rays of light before the infinite darkness; and Larry found it, Eureka!, found his cousin's diary complete with entries demystifying their final days, explaining what went wrong (in fact, they had turned back to rejoin the main party not long after they separated, but they soon fell ill and their camels, also in bad shape, escaped; without food, water or shelter they expired while trying to catch up), why they did what they did, and what should be said to whom. Miraculous that Larry found it, even if the pair did perish on the main track (which, incidentally, was not searched for a very long time), for not only were the bodies left exposed to the elements but there were also the animals to consider; perhaps it was testament to their depleted physical condition that the wild dogs and other carnivores left Charles Wells and George Jones well enough alone for the six months between their demise and Larry and his men appearing on the scene, there was nothing left on their bones worth tucking into; what melancholy happiness Larry must have felt on locating his missing cousin, the man who he, as leader of the expedition, was supposed to protect, what closure seeing and handling those bodies must have brought him, a sudden extinguishing of the sick guilt-type feeling of not knowing, the claustrophobic panic of disorientation, the madness of a hyperactive imagination, what liberty, sadness and relief Larry must have found out there in the Great Sandy Desert, where they thought there was absolutely nothing to be found, Lawrence Allen 'Larry' Wells found closure and peace of mind in the form of his cousin's body and diary, and thus he could go on with his life—not as simply as before, no, but still with a huge preoccupation, a nauseating insanity boring into his guts day after day after day, finally wrapped up and packed away by the last words of his ill-fated cousin—he could go on with his life as what many described as "the Last Australian Explorer," which he did for decades thereafter, and while the search for Charles and George was, in the end, successful—if one might consider finding their sun-dried bodies successful—the Calvert Expedition was not the roaring success they'd hoped it would be, for among their unachieved goals of opening a stock route between the Northern Territory and the West Australian goldfields, charting the unknown Great Sandy Desert and the collection of scientific specimens, they had also hoped to find evidence of the fate of another troupe, that of the lost Leichhardt Expedition of 1848, led by the German explorer and naturalist Friedrich Wilhelm 'Ludwig' Leichhardt, who endeavoured to take his party from the Condamine River in Queensland northwest to Port Essington then south and west through the deserts of the Northern Territory and Western Australia to Swan River on the West Australian coast, a journey that would take him across the entire continent and supposedly take between two and three years, which is why Leichhardt's expedition consisted of five Europeans, two Aboriginal guides, seven horses, twenty mules and fifty bullocks, quite the company it must be said, all of which vanished without a trace having last been seen at Cogoon on the Darling Downs, not a bone, not a cigar case was found, leading to a multitude of search parties over the following century-and-a-half (and an equal number of theories and suppositions), each intent on solving one of the great Australian mysteries of what exactly happened to Ludwig Leichhardt and his considerable expedition, someone must know something—there have been, as you might expect, several theories that have come down through the intervening years: that he and his company were caught by the floodwaters of the Cooper River that crosses from Queensland to South Australia (incidentally it was the Cooper where the nation's most famous explorers, Robert O'Hara Burke and William John Wills, lost their lives); that his company was attacked and killed by a native tribe (thanks to stories passed around by other explorers from tribes with which they were friendly); or that, according to one Joseph Anderson Panton, painter, etcher and police magistrate, as well as expert on all things Leichhardt, the company had perished in the middle of the Great Sandy Desert, a theory based on his finding "the camp of a white man" at Elsey Creek in the Northern Territory not long after Leichhardt's disappearance; in fact, David Carnegie himself, while on his expedition to Halls Creek almost forty years later, came across a native tribe who showed him some items they had in their possession—an iron tent peg, the lid of a matchbox and a clasp from a saddle—items Carnegie thought may have belonged to the ill-fated German naturalist, for even by the late nineteenth century some of these things, particularly the iron tent peg, were no longer in use (too heavy). And so while Larry Wells' explorations failed to find anything that might have shed light on the disappearance of Ludwig Leichhardt and his crew, they did ultimately lead him to the body and diary of his lost cousin Charles, and perhaps this was the greatest boon of all, because now he could carry news back to his family and the guilt he undoubtedly felt as a result of losing one of his company (a relative, no less) could be in some part assuaged by the knowledge held in that diary and the closure it provided, which in a sense drew an indelible line under the life of Charles Wells, brought him back to his loved ones and kept him tucked up in the cradle of their affections, as opposed to spinning off in the æther of open-ended unknowing, a state in which I found myself for a long time, particularly in the time before Johnny Bègue stumbled across the flaperon, wherein I often found myself expect-

ing Alison and Beatrice to show up on our doorstep, or to be crossing the street in town (I saw their faces every time I stepped out of
the house), or to somehow simply appear, a situation that brought
me to the edge of sanity on more than one occasion. Standing in
that Cathedral of Knowing, in that vast high-ceilinged chamber deep
in the old Prince of Wales goldmine just outside of Coolgardie, the
idea that we were on the cusp of a great invasion of knowledge
filled me with hope and positivity; these were the dying days of
the unknown, the last gasp of not knowing, heralding the age of
information in which every fact, datum or titbit is literally at our
fingertips, the time of light at the end of the tunnel, of banished
darkness, a time in which the great illusionist, escapologist and
mesmeriser, Ehrich Weisz, the Handcuff King, would be turning in
his early grave, for he was insistent on keeping the mystery alive,
on keeping wonder alive, even though he would stand before his
audiences and maintain, "This is mere trickery and sleight of hand.
There is no magic!" his was a craft like anything else, like ship-
building, like aeronautic engineering, it was all mechanics and nothing more, though even then he was always careful to never give
away his secrets, how he did it, he wanted to own and guard the
mystery; which was why, as vaudeville fell out of favour, Houdini
took to travelling the globe debunking supposed spiritualists, setting out to explain in his lectures exactly how each got away with
his or her fraudulent acts—the most famous being Lady Jean Doyle
(wife of Sir Arthur Conan) who claimed to have "reached" Houdini's
beloved mother several years after the latter's passing, a claim
that the great Harry was happy to go along with for the sake of the
friendship, but one that he ultimately debunked, much to the fury
of the scientific Sir Arthur (who Harry thought "a bit senile" and
easily "bamboozled"), with one simple fact: his mother didn't speak
English, therefore why would she "reach out" via a twenty-three
page letter "in classical English," a language she'd never used with
him before?, which is to say that Harry, Ehrich, Erik wanted know-

ledge, but he was not democratic with it, he knew it was the key to success, but he wanted it all to himself, for he was very well aware that if you control knowledge you control mystery, and without mystery one could say goodbye to bums on seats, because he likewise knew very well that were anyone to cotton on to his heroics, they would simply clasp their hands over their stomachs, lean back and say, "Ah, well *that* makes sense then," and this would be the death of mystery, the death of wonder, a double-edged sword, but one that I, Arthur Bernard Cripp (Bernard to those who know me) would happily wield, come what may!, for I would happily put all awe and wonder to bed for the sake of complete knowledge— give me the apple and I'll take a whopping bite out of it—Houdini would be aghast at the concept of the YouTube tutorial, but I welcomed it, with open arms I ran towards the age of absolute knowing, I'd have us fill up every underground tunnel, every old mine, every cave, every hidden source of water, pack them full of blinking servers, racks and racks of hard drives, ship them out to the desert in a never-ending convoy of roadtrains, bring on the great debunking, wonder be damned, for as long as there was hope that we were on the brink of the age of knowing, I could forestall to some degree the anxiety of not knowing, and the idea that the barren and cutthroat Australian deserts could one day hum with all the knowledge of history, of everything down to the last detail, down to where you and I buy our groceries, down to what meals we prepare with these groceries, made me well up with gratitude, gratitude towards Vasily for bringing me here, yes, gratitude towards those many diggers who broke their backs against the rock that was surrounding us, the explorers and proprietors, pioneers and prospectors who, powered by hope, funded by luck, opened up this underground network, who undertook the bone-shattering work of boring and blasting their way down here and conceiving space within space, *terra nullius* within *terra nullius*, as though by force of some obscure and brilliant mathematical equation these diggers had solved the unutterable problem of dividing oblivion by itself, for they'd excavated the King of Metals, they'd exhausted the landscape, seemingly laid it to waste and moved on, but now instead of taking it out, this new breed of diggers would replace that gold with all the information known to humankind, a new underground network traversing the known desert, and I for one welcomed it with open arms and felt, for the first time in almost two years, an inkling of joy. Now, I do not know if this was Vasily's objective in bringing me to that renovation, I never did ask him; perhaps he had simply taken it upon himself to distract me, to provide me with something to do during those long days between nighttime performances, to keep my mind occupied and away from subjects that were traumatic for me, but whether it was his intention or not, he gave me a gift that has carried me through the intervening years: a love for and faith in information, *knowing*, a love of digging up facts, unearthing truths, or at least searching for them, seeking them out, of getting wind of a potential boon and setting off into the great unknown, for it is there that I will find my treasure, my fortune, it is only there that I will find more than traces, more than the odd flaperon or elusive handshake, but real treasure, hard evidence, immovable facts, irrefutable, nestled in among all the ephemera, the inconclusive, the incorrect, the speculative and not-to-be-trusted, actual co-ordinates instead of hazy hemispheres and abstract vortex zones, all of which in the end lead to a story, a narrative, which in turn has meaning; whatever his motivation, I have my dear friend to thank for giving me hope when I'd run out completely, and it is a friendship I will treasure for all time. And so I emerged from the old Prince of Wales mine, blinking into the heat and clouds of flies on the fringes of the West Australian desert, a different Arthur Bernard Cripp, Bernard to those who know me, something had fired, a switch had been tripped, and from that moment on I began a process of collecting and recording—either physically or at the very least mentally—every detail I could, every skerrick of information that made its way to me or that I actively sought out, for it is not deeds or endeavours upon which our lives and our nations are built, it is information, now more so than ever; it was an appetite not so much for the facts themselves, but for the stories they engendered, because stories carry degrees of meaning, they are the gravity of existence, enabling us, our histories, to take shape, in short to make sense of the chaos; a case in point being that knowing Ehrich Weiss, Harry Houdini, was in fact not the first but the second person in history to conduct a controlled flight in a powered aircraft over Australian soil is seemingly more important than knowing who *was* the first; perhaps it is because, in this age of infinite information, it is much easier and more obvious to know who was first and therefore reflects a keener intellect and more tenacious investigation in knowing who was *second*, this is more valuable information for it is not as easily found, the rules of scarcity still apply, and it suggests a more nuanced understanding of history, a subtler dealing with the facts and thus a richer and more complete reality, not to mention a greater capacity to deal with life's ups and downs—could we be heading towards a world in which winning is not the be-all and end-all? could it be that coming in second will outstrip coming in first?—and so the Arthur Bernard Cripp that emerged from the old Prince of Wales mine to continue with that eleven-month, somewhat ramshackle tour of regional Australia—taking in Kalgoorlie (we managed to relocate after three shows in Coolgardie), Esperance, Albany, Margaret River, Fremantle, Perth, Geraldton, Mount Magnet (another slip-up on Vasily's part), Alice Springs, Oodnadatta, Coober Pedy, Broken Hill, Birdsville, Charleville, Cunnamulla, Bourke, Dubbo and Wagga Wagga—was an Arthur Bernard Cripp with an insatiable thirst for knowledge and its curative powers— for, despite my spiritual experience in the Prince of Wales mine, I did after all still need curing; in fact, now that I think about it, it is likely that my need for curing prompted my spiritual experience, or at least opened me to having one—and day after day, after a night of setting myself on fire in front of hundreds of mesmerised faces, I endeavoured to learn as much as I could in every town, at every stop, to take on as much information as possible, to inhale it, to draw it down inside me like those bunkers that are being filled with mountains of data; and I guess what goes in must come out, for on the journey back to Melbourne after our final show in Wagga, we stopped at a roadhouse just outside the little town of Diggers Rest for coffee and a toilet break—it was only half-an-hour to the city, but the traffic was going to be murder—and it was there that some-one made mention to me of the fact of Houdini's historic flight in a nearby paddock—really it was not more than a passing comment—but with my newfound spirit I managed to convince the driver to take us by the spot so that we could see the plaque which I duly photographed and here reproduce:

It was an image—or, rather, an idea—that remained seared into my memory for the ensuing months, and while it took some time for me to admit to my desire to recreate Houdini's famous flight, I believe

I had made up my mind to do so the split-second I took that picture on that sunny afternoon at the end of winter; on a practical level, I also needed something to occupy me, a project, now that the tour was finished, something to direct my mind and prevent it from spiralling off in any number of other directions as it has become increasingly prone to doing; it's as if the more I know, the more information I acquire, the hungrier I am to know more, to go further, deeper, in any particular direction, and if it weren't for the Houdini flight, for the need to get it absolutely right in every detail down to the journalist with pad and pencil and *Argus* staff photographer with his Kodak Brownie No. 2 looking up in awe as I took off and swooped overhead above the old Plumpton paddock exactly as it is in the photograph, a miraculous feat in itself, a complete re-creation—pure theatre, you might say, a stunt, a gimmick, and you'd be correct, an elaborate staged performance, yes, but this did not detract from the project, not in the slightest, because in fact *the original feat was also an act of pure theatre*, a stunt, a gimmick, not to mention the fact that it was perpetrated by a man famous for his stunts, tricks, illusions and gimmicks, the Great Harry Houdini, for whom his flight at Diggers Rest on Friday 18 March 1910 at eight in the morning was not an attempt to be the first person to conduct a controlled flight in a powered aircraft over Australian soil—it was, but it wasn't—the record was important but only insofar as it was a means to a greater end, which was promoting The Legend of Harry Houdini; at a time when aviation was sweeping the globe and interest was soaring—many newspapers had their own dedicated section entitled 'Flight' that featured news of aviation attempts from around the globe—Erik Weisz, Ehrich Weiss, Harry Houdini was climbing aboard a steamer to travel to the far reaches of the earth, to deepest darkest Diggers Rest, to conduct the first ever flight there, which at the time was headline-grabbing stuff, and he knew it, which is to say that the record was important to Houdini, not because he was a serious aviator, but in that it would add to the allure and mystique of his name, for that was always the end: the name, everything boiled down to the name, his journey Down Under included; all of it, a publicity stunt, which of course bears negative connotations, but I for one did not begrudge him it, not in the slightest, for it only served to lend greater authenticity to my own attempt; like Houdini, I was not a serious aviator, nor did I have much interest in flying anything afterwards—indeed, after leaving Australia, Houdini never took to the skies again—all that mattered to me, like the Handcuff King, was Diggers Rest, and it was an idea that took root as we left that little plaque near the old Plumpton paddock and headed back along the Tullamarine Freeway towards the city centre to complete a very roundabout, misshapen circuit of our country, whereafter I moved in with my father, whose condition had deteriorated greatly in my absence; he had trouble recognising me and recalling how I fit into his life, and now does not recognise me at all, for he is calling out again, this time for his wife, my mother, the clairvoyant who died many years ago, and when I get up from my writing desk and go into him, to calm him, my presence only makes him more agitated because he does not understand why when he calls out my mother's name—"Marigold!"—I am the one to appear—"Not you! I said Marigold!"—and so I try to divert his attention to the circus, *his* circus, the one he took over from his adoptive parents, the one that brought so many people so much happiness, so much entertainment and diversion, the momentary respite that comes with feelings of awe and wonder, of being decoupled from the gravity of existence, that floating feeling when you are completely overcome by what you are seeing unfold before your very eyes, that thing that does not quite make sense and yet here it is and you say "How is that possible? How can that be?!" with a sort of drunken drawl in your voice, very similar to the one with which my father, Arthur, speaks now, that kind of mystified timbre of his voice and shape of his words together with that bewildered look in his eyes—an expression he spent a lifetime trading in and now here it is, his permanent state, heartbreaking but in a way poetic; he does not seem to suffer apart from his occasional bad dreams and the confusion when he cries out for his wife, but when I tell him about his circus, about his life spent as ringmaster, travelling all over, the clarity returns and he speaks with purpose and recall, often reiterating his own refrain: "We have to give the people what they cannot get from television!" which was his primary concern when he took over from his parents in the mid-1960s—I wonder what he would now make of the internet and what it has meant for our circus, what it is doing to our brains, but of course I don't mention it—and it is only after we've been talking about the circus for twenty minutes that he recognises me, remembers me, and says with that all-too-familiar mischievous sparkle in his eye and tone of voice of someone reading a fairytale, "Bernard! My boy. A miracle; they said we couldn't have children, they were certain of it!" every time, without fail, "The Incredible Man of Fire!" he says, and then, "We gave them something they couldn't get from the idiot box with you, boy," and he takes my hand in his, his skin is like dry, thin translucent paper, and almost squeezes; it is the same routine, every time, every day, the act of forgetting and remembering, and every day it is as though he's remembering it all for the first time; there seems to be genuine pleasure there, but inevitably his memory will hit upon a raw nerve, maybe an image of my mother, maybe his days of running the business—it is a tender blessing that he's remained oblivious to what happened to his daughter-in-law and granddaughter; or, at least, he never mentions it and nor do I—and he retreats back into the fog of unknowing, the blanket of obliviousness, and when I try once again to remind him of who he was and what he did he looks at me flatly and mumbles, "Did I?" and gives a "hmph!" as though he is not at all surprised at his own folly, neither surprised nor any longer interested, and I'm not completely convinced there isn't a part of his will that's in command of opening and closing this window to the past, a part that is not fully conscious but also not *not* conscious either, which can be hurtful and frustrating at times, but if I am honest who *wouldn't* want that particular power? to burn it all up, to extinguish it all, the last days of knowing, for if we can't know absolutely everything what point is there in knowing anything at all? surely it's worse, ie. more painful, to know only part of the picture—indeed it is, I can tell you!—and so it makes me wonder whether my own excavations into the mountains of knowledge we as a race have amassed aren't motivated by the same impulse, that all this gathering together, recording, setting down, ordering, isn't in fact an act of forgetting, of erasure, of painting the face of chaos when all is in fact disorder, atrophy and decay, when information only ever comes after the fact and comprises a sort of retroactive shield against an enemy that is already through the gates, which is to say that perhaps it is best to not know and to gaze in awe and wonder and terror; I shouldn't dwell on that side of things, however, for if I were to do that I'd stop and if I stop... well, I can't stop, there's no stopping, not now, best to keep going, keep thinking, collecting, writing, getting the story down, best to keep talking and never break the thread, to keep searching and, who knows, who knows what I will find, just remember our good friend Johnny Bègue, who was merely searching for a rock with which to grind chilies, on a beach that was littered with rocks,

really it wasn't even a search, *per se*, for look at all those rocks, any of which would do a wonderful job of grinding chillies, any one at all; a search implies scarcity and real effort, thinking, planning, co-ordinating, elusiveness, not abundance, it implies that something is *missing*, but look: imagine searching for a rock on that beach; impossible!—his search was over before it began; no wonder his mind moved on to other things—surely it was that or go mad—and his curiosity was piqued, not by potential specimens for his kitchen, but by something sticking up from between the rocks, something alien, the silver of the shorn metal gleaming in the tropical sun, winking at him, calling him to it; now, I do not consider myself a philosopher or towering intellect—though I do believe intelligence and empathy go hand-in-hand, so I try to use my mind as much as possible—but I have thought about Johnny Bègue's miraculous discovery a lot, of course I have, and I wonder if the sheer volume of suitable rocks on that Réunion beach was in fact *the* contributing factor to his finding that flaperon, for instead of simply reaching down and picking up the first rock to hand, he gazed out over that stretch of beach which contained a mind-numbing variety of candidates and this had the effect of putting him into a hesitant, even trancelike, state, meaning that for a while he stood there with the tiny waves whispering through the stones, the calls of the birds, the brine in the air, the humidity on his brow, really the sheer abundance stunned him into a meditative state, and the only thing that could retrieve him from it was anything there that was *not* a stone, in this case the ripped-off flaperon from the doomed MH370 with its two hundred and thirty-nine souls onboard, as though all the stones rose up as a sort of choir singing a transporting hymn, something so haunting that it caused his mind to shift into another dimension or level of consciousness, a door was blown wide open, and there lay the only piece of hard evidence in known existence of the fate of that flight (since the discovery of the flaperon, there have been two other discoveries categorised by the authorities as "definitely belonging to MH370"—a left outboard flap trailing edge and a right outboard flap—five "almost certainly belonging to MH370"—a flap track fairing, horizontal stabiliser panel, engine nose cowling segment, closet panel, and a cabin interior panel—and about twenty-five other fragments that "likely belong to MH370"), miraculous really that tonnes of rocks could have the effect of relieving him from the gravity of the everyday, but there you are, for if there had been only one or two rocks down on that beach who knows what might have happened, that scrap of metal might have gone unnoticed and the next day been completely covered in sand forever, for our beachcomber would simply have scooped up that suitable crushing stone and returned home without a thought for anything else other than the way chilli teases out the flavours of his favourite dishes. And so I will not, cannot, stop searching, will not and cannot cease writing, for who knows what I might stumble across, who knows what I might find, what might emerge gleaming from the rubble; besides, now that I have wound up Cripp's Circus—that final tour of regional towns failed to save us, in part thanks to the exorbitant costs of having to travel such vast distances for such small audiences—and my days are now spent caring for Dad, there is little else for me other than to train my mind on the task at hand—either that or go mad—in the hope of bringing some sort of coherence to it all, some closure, some *sense*; I did entertain the idea of simply going on forever, of writing without end, writing to end all writing for it would contain everything possible, every story, every character, every scenario, every setting that anyone could ever dream up; the idea of spending the rest of my life writing page after page after page, of *never* bringing it to a close, I could just keep going forever, an infinite labyrinth that opened into more and more tunnels, from story to story, it would never have to end; I could even find someone to take over from me when the time came, when I died suddenly from heart failure or in a car crash, or when my mind started to go and I no longer remembered how to distinguish between d's and b's, or when I mixed up the meanings behind simple words like "rock" or "spice" and the sentences fell into complete gibberish; I could have waited for the day when I sat down here at my desk and simply stared at the letters on my keyboard like Johnny Bègue staring out across his abundance of stones, unable to decide on any one in particular, unable to attach any meaning to any of them; on that day I could have called in someone else, someone much younger, who could take over the story and who in turn, when the time was right, would pass it on, so that the narrative would not be dependent on any one life in particular but could go on and on; which of course would require a reader (or readers) to follow suit, to sit and read, day after day, and then when their eyes failed them, to pass it on in a similar fashion—just imagine it going on forever so that no-one could ever know it all, for we simply do not have the technology to a) keep us alive indefinitely or b) instantaneously implant the entire novel (though it would never *be* entire) into the reader's mind, which would in any case defeat the purpose of the novel, besides which I fear, perhaps more than my fear of finishing, the reader's wrath or, worse, indifference, which would be, for me, like the poison dart with David Wynford Carnegie's name on it, for it is one thing to arrest the reader, but it is quite another to hold them hostage, and so what am I to do but cut the thread, for to indulge myself would be, for the reader, something like getting on an aircraft and never getting off, like boarding an infinite flight that no radar could hope to track forever, or it could even be something like waiting for an aircraft that never arrives despite the arrivals board showing it *en route*, despite announcements made to the contrary saying that Flight Such-and-Such will arrive at Such-and-Such a time at Such-and-Such a gate but it never does, it just keeps arriving forever, *ad infinitum*, and while this is the feeling I carry in my heart, day in day out, in my waking life and in my dreams, I would not wish it upon anyone ever, not even on whatever force is responsible for fate and coincidence, and so rather than perpetuate it, I will create the closure I cannot have, find the courage I do not have, and bring things to a satisfactory end. After returning from that tour of regional Australia, which was the final nail in the coffin for Cripp's Circus, family enterprise going on almost a century, passed from father to son, father to son; after seeing the plaque at Diggers Rest commemorating the (mistaken) fact that Harry Houdini was the first person in history to conduct a controlled flight in a powered aircraft over Australian soil, I allowed to grow inside me an image of a recreation of that event, an image of myself astride the controls in that basic (though for the times quite advanced) machine, which admittedly resembled an elaborate bicycle with a boxtail, looking down at the trees blurring below me, the disinterested horses chewing the grass, and the small knot of men looking up as I ascend, ascend, ascend to a height of around thirty metres and make several deliberate turns during my two hundred and twenty-five-second flight (Houdini made three flights on that fateful day: the first under a minute, then another two, the longest of which was 3m45sec, and it was this one I wished to emulate) before making a somewhat bumpy but triumphant landing, skidding across tussock and dung to the cheers of the onlookers, the resigned, wounded smile from a defeated Ralph C. Banks/H.C. L'Oste Rolfe—who is indeed living up to his *nom du pilote* having now lost the race to the record—and my good friend and mechanic whose first and last concern is not for me but for his beloved aircraft, which he will run towards before I've even come to a complete stop in order to ensure I haven't damaged anything in coming down so hard—the image, or rather images, came to me fully formed, though exactly when is difficult to say because by the time I was aware of them it seemed as though they were already a part of who I was, as though I'd seen it before, though before my first trip to Diggers Rest if you had asked me who was Australia's first aviator I would not have been able to tell you, and yet that image was like something from a recurring dream, a dream about which I'd forgotten only to realise upon remembering that it was entirely familiar to me, maybe something like the sudden clearing of amnesia, or even amnesia in reverse, the curtain lifted and there it was, the paddock, the Voisin biplane, the man sitting upright at the controls—the man, of course, being Houdini, being me—the *Argus* reporter, the photographer with his Kodak Brownie No. 2, all of it, there it was, and the more I learned about the whole episode the more detailed the image became, so that by the time I reached out to Francis 'Southy' Southermore, former British Rail conductor and model aircraft enthusiast, who massaged the stump of his left leg with the expression of a saint receiving the stigmata, with the request to construct for me a 1:1 scale version of the Voisin that Houdini had piloted into the history books, I was so immersed in this moment in my country's past that I was barely in my own time at all; I'd become something of an anachronism, for I changed the way I wore my hair and clothes, preferring to reflect the way Houdini wore his, hair parted down the middle, suits and ties, newspaper boy hat turned backwards, not every day but increasingly as time went by and Southy's machine came into being, a machine over which he laboured if not daily then several times every week at that huge storage facility near Tullamarine Airport. I took the affectation of my appearance to heart, as might an actor preparing for a role, for in order to do the recreation any justice at all, in order to bring it to life and engender it with a degree of authenticity, I needed to walk, as it were, in Ehrich Weiss's derbies, spats and all, I needed to be able to look down and see myself in clothes I would not normally wear and imagine myself into a time to which I did not belong—or perhaps it was the case that I belonged to that time more than my own— which is to say that in order to do the project properly I had to, as much as I could, *become* Harry Houdini, pull on his skin, as it were, so that when eventually I took to the skies in his Voisin—not the original, of course, for it is now lost, but Southy's replica—I might touch something, a feeling, a moment, a waypoint in a time of wonders and miracles, when history could be made and time did not stand still, when one could leap forth into the unknown, when finding and discovery were still possible, when there were still explorable pockets of the earth, when one could be Prince of the Air, to be in the air was majestic and rare, as rare as the King of Metals, so rare that going up in any kind of machine was a newsworthy occurrence, stories about which one could locate in the 'Flights' section of the paper and read about all the new attempts at various records, winners of air races, new inventions and agreements the world over, a time before this time of illusions, when clouds were in the skies and we knew what we knew and we also knew what we didn't know, a time before it was all jumbled up and turned on its head, a time before we walked upside down, I could reach out and touch it, or rather like in those science fiction movies I could fly right into it in a flash of light and a trail of fire and emerge, *poof!*, in the Diggers Rest of some hundred years before, looking down over one of my dipping wings and seeing the flashbulb on the Kodak Brownie No. 2 going off as I throw out a wave, an image that would go down in history, a time in which a miracle was a machine getting up, up, up into the air as opposed to vanishing completely from it. I would not receive any flying lessons—nothing official, at any rate, from an accredited organisation or governing body—for Houdini's training merely included tips from Brassac (himself a prizewinning pilot), the observations of others, and a lot of trial and error; besides, there were barely any airfields in those days, let alone flight schools, so you had to learn on the job, as it were, a style of learning that I was more than happy to embrace because after winding up the circus, my only source of income was the carer's allowance I received for looking after my father, and flight school is immensely expensive, prohibitively so, especially when any money I did have was going towards building the Voisin, which meant that, while the aircraft was under construction, I busily and dutifully read everything I could get my hands on with regard to operating the biplane, as well as watching every clip I could find online (of which there are a surprising abundance from the time Houdini was in Australia) in an effort to familiarise myself with everything from the steering to the fuel to the engine, everything, including general principles of aviation that could be important to know when you are some thirty metres off the ground, and so while Southy worked on the mechanical side of things on his workshop floor, I could often be found up at his workbench trawling through whatever resources I could access, and then cross-checking my information with what-ever part of the aircraft Southy happened to be working on at the time. Though really it was quite simple: to ascend you pushed the steering wheel forwards and to descend you pulled it backwards; you controlled the rudder via a foot pedal and there was a little choke at the side of the steering wheel that regulated fuel flow to the engine; as for the structural make-up of the machine, it was something like a huge boxkite with the fuselage section measuring thirty-three feet long by about six wide, with a wingspan of also thirty-three feet; these wings were at the very front of the aircraft, extending out either side of the pilot's shoulders and it was like sitting inside an elaborate lantern divided into several translucent sections; the tail was a single boxlike structure, with a wheel at its base and housing the rudder system, all of which was attached to the front section via a series of outriggers and functioned to both stabilise and steer the machine; powering it was a water-cooled E.N.V. engine (named after the French phrase *en-V* describing the structure of the motor and how it was "in a V," though surely it was also a nod towards the English word "envy," an emotion that was undoubtedly driving the race skywards at the time), which was capable of generating up to eighty horsepower and could get the eight-foot steel-shafted propeller spinning at around 1200 revolutions per minute, which is to say that, at heart, it was like a mongrel crossbred elongated tricycle with wings and a motor—hardly something you'd need a license for, the kind of contraption you'd build in your garage and take for a spin at the local park; the miracle was not only that it was capable of flight, but that something like this marked such a significant moment in Australian aviation. And perhaps, for Harry Houdini, Erik Weisz, that was the point; the more unlikely the stunt was to succeed, the more value it had as a promotional tool; the more death-defying, the more unfathomable, the greater the attention he could command, but although this is undoubtedly true, one must always remember that the Voisin and especially the E.N.V. motor were at the time the very cutting edge of technology which in today's money would be something like the worldwide network of telescopic cameras they used to capture the first image of a black hole, and in tomorrow's money who knows, maybe it will be something like using fibreoptics to transport consciousness faster than the speed of light back in time; but in February 1910 at Diggers Rest, in a huge marquee that resembled a diminutive circus bigtop, the diminutive French mechanic, Antonio Brassac, was painstakingly assembling the Voisin that had arrived in pieces with the Great Houdini, for whom Brassac awoke before dawn and checked and double-checked and triple-checked that everything was in order so that when the Master's town car came bouncing through the old Plumpton paddock as the sun came up all would be set for an attempt at the record, and day after day after day when the Master emerged from his vehicle looking increasingly drawn and bleary-eyed (Australia was not a good time for Houdini, who by now had reached the summit of his powers and was beginning to become increasingly introspective), Brassac would strike his telltale match and, on seeing the mesmerising snakelike swagger of the smoke twisting on the air, would exclaim yet again

"*Beaucoup de vent! Beaucoup de vent!*" and Houdini would sigh, look to the skies like a curmudgeon shaking his fist and cursing this wretched place, so far south as to be on hell's doorstep, with weather to match, and say to his beloved mechanic that the miracle won't be getting the record, nor will it be getting man and machine in the air, the miracle will be the calming of the winds that seemed to rush perpetually across this damned plain, to which Brassac would say with a grin that surely such a force of nature as the Great Houdini ought to be able to influence such things, to which Erik Weisz would reply almost beneath his breath that, yes, there was a time when he might have been able to do just that; but now, at only thirty-six, Houdini, greying hair mussed by the gusting winds, body aching and vaudeville on the way out, was beginning to ask himself questions, and after speaking wistfully he turned with the aching gravity of a man more than twice his age—his body having been pushed and pulled, wrung and tortured for two decades—and levered himself into the back seat of the town car and breathed out an instruction to his driver to head back to the city, "Too dangerous today," leaving Brassac to fuss over the aircraft, to acquire a better understanding of the air's characteristics in this part of the world, and to wonder whether his friend and employer was not starting to at last feel the fear that had been waiting in the wings for so many years. Because Houdini had found misfortune barely three months before in Hamburg, at the Hufaren military parade grounds in Wandsbek to be precise—back then air travel was practically non-existent, which meant that so were airfields, hence the use of the Plumpton paddock at Diggers Rest—it was mid-November 1909 and the vast flat field was exposed to the tempestuous advances of the closing German winter, storms, sleet and icy winds cutting across the temporary runway to make take-off impossible and relegating Houdini to sitting at the controls in a nearby shed which he'd rented to serve as a hangar, practicing his launch protocols, listening to Brassac's enthusiastic, obsessive instructions, and no doubt, somewhere in the back of his mind, beyond even the fear he was doing his best to stifle, was the seed of that winter-blooming flower of knowledge, knowledge that despite who he was, despite what he had done—perhaps even *because* of what he had done, the self-torture, the extremes to which he'd driven himself, the chainings, the near-drownings, being frozen half to death, broken bones and blackened eyes and blistered skin—these stunts could not go on forever, or rather *he* could not go on forever—he did not believe in the afterlife, despite wanting to: he had found no proof, and nor would he—for so long as technology advanced and humankind pushed the limits of everything, there would always be new frontiers, new limits to define the extreme, limits much like our universe, always and forever expanding, but one man, regardless of who he was, could not hope to stay at the limit forever, could not hope to stay there even for two decades, twenty years was starting to push it, which is to say that, like an elite athlete whose body has been their vehicle to success, the vehicle that has given their existence meaning, he was not infallible, that the will to be first takes its toll and the body will always have its revenge, and so while the Great Houdini was caught up in the hype and hysteria around flight, swept up in his own obsession with capitalising on it, to be among the first in the world to take to the skies—not to mention being the first in Australia to complete a controlled flight in a powered aircraft—he was also, as he sat at the controls of his newly bought Voisin in that cobbled-together hangar looking out toward the bleak Hufaren military parade grounds near Hamburg, beginning to worry about the future; how much more could he withstand? how much longer could he go on torturing himself? was this the beginning of the end? which part of himself would ultimately win out, the whipper or the whipped? and would there be a place in the world for the one who survived? Maybe it was these thoughts that, although nascent, added extra weight to the cockpit;

perhaps it was the effort required to ignore them that diminished his capacity to focus, or it could have simply been because it was his first time going up in an aircraft; whatever the case, when at last they got a clear, still day that late autumn and the Voisin was rolled out of its hangar and onto the parade grounds, with officers of the German Army gathered around to see, Houdini lowered his goggles and set off, taxiing along the bumpy earth before easing the steering wheel forward in order to generate lift and thus bringing a cheer from the onlooking soldiers who could only but marvel at what they were seeing, the dawn of a new era, real progress, excitement for the future; but it was unfortunately an excitement short-lived, for after barely ten seconds—was it a gust of wind or pilot error?—the machine's attitude changed suddenly and almost before anyone knew what was happening, while the cheers and hoots still hung in the air, the cunning escape artist found himself in a nose-dive, one that was, due to his lack of altitude, unassailable, and he was pitched head-on into the earth, destroying the propeller and smashing up the front end of the aircraft. It was the kind of accident that was particularly dangerous for a pilot, given that he was positioned at the very front of the machine, the propeller could easily come flying forward—back then it was positioned behind the cockpit—or the pilot could simply be thrown headlong into whatever the plane had hit, but as fortune would have it Houdini walked away with barely a scratch, leaving Brassac, aghast at his pride and joy being almost completely destroyed (luckily, the engine and rudder were undamaged), to rebuild the front end before another, more successful attempt several weeks later on 26 November when the Master managed to achieve lift-off and remain in flight long enough for the photographers to capture it, the evidence of which the great magician, illusionist and self-promoter disseminated to newspapers worldwide. And while it was his reputation and image that Houdini was advertising explicitly, there was a tacit, implicit motivation not only to his first flights in Hamburg, but also to his travelling to Australia with Brassac and the Voisin, for behind the scenes—in fact, behind most aviation attempts in Europe at the time—lurked the shadowy figure of a certain Alfred Charles Harmsworth, who later bought and used the title Lord Northcliffe, 1st Viscount of Northcliffe, an Irish newspaper magnate and later Director for Propaganda who, in the early part of the twentieth century, through owning and controlling both the *Daily Mail* and the *Daily Mirror*, exerted a huge influence on public opinion and was, according to some, "the greatest figure to ever walk down Fleet Street"; he also used his considerable clout to promote a fierce anti-German sentiment that left some to exclaim: "Next to the Kaiser, Lord Northcliffe [did] more than any living man to bring about the war." As Northcliffe's wealth and power grew, one of his major frustrations was his government's sluggish attitude towards aviation, which he perceived as a glaring weakness in military defence; sensing that controlled, powered flight would play a major role in any future international conflict (indeed, the one he was fuelling), Northcliffe tried via contacts within government to get military people to the airshows that were cropping up with increasing frequency around the world, for if they could only see what other countries (including Germany, which was already embracing this new technology) were achieving, he was certain Britain would stop dragging her heels and start taking these new developments seriously; but even his good friend Lord Haldane, 1st Viscount Haldane aka Richard Burdon Haldane, politician, lawyer, philosopher, Knight of the Thistle, and Secretary of State for War—a multilingual Scot who possessed the unfortunate dichotomy of having a passion for both the British Empire and German culture—even Lord Haldane was unmoved by Northcliffe's entreaties regarding aviation, and so the increasingly powerful media man took matters into his own hands, which is to say that, via his newspapers, he began offering considerable cash prizes for certain completed flights that by 1916 had amounted to around USD $95,000, including rewards for such feats as the first cross-Channel flight, a race around Britain, the first London to Manchester flight, and one of the first model aeroplane competitions. At the end of 1909, while Harry Houdini was dusting himself off after his Hamburg crash, Northcliffe, a close friend of Houdini's, was starting to generate significant publicity; hearing of his friend's intentions towards aviation, it is said that Northcliffe seized the opportunity to generate even more interest in the cause and therefore "encouraged" the great man—one can only assume this "encouragement" referred to obliquely by several sources meant either cash or publicity via Northcliffe's many publications; one suspects the latter, for such publicity would have served the interests of both men—Northcliffe "encouraged" Houdini to make the long journey south and become the first person to conduct a controlled flight in a powered aircraft over Australian soil, a stunt that would undoubtedly whip up a sensation; the image alone would get tongues wagging: the great mechanical bird with the word HOUDINI in massive letters down the side had front page written all over it. No doubt the 1st Viscount of Northcliffe also realised the strategic significance of Australia to the Commonwealth given its proximity to Japan which, it was said, was already, like the Germans, in the throes of constructing an aviation corps, and was not only learning all things flight from Germany but also commissioning a construction and repair station, which is to say that if Australia was a great spot from which to keep the Japanese in check, on the other side of the coin it was also vulnerable to attack from them, a concern that made its way into the headlines of Australian newspapers immediately following the roaring success of Houdini's endeavours Down Under and drove great changes within the Australian defence forces, for no less than a year later Lieutenant George Taylor of the Australian Intelligence Corps penned a twenty-page booklet that was duly published by the Aerial

League of Australia under the title 'Wanted at Once! An Aerial Defence Fleet for Australia – A National Call to Australians,' they were really shouting it from the rooftops, and with all thanks to—or at least in large part because of—Houdini's knack for self-promotion—Houdini, that is, *and* the indefatigable vaudeville promotor, performance venue proprietor, renowned baritone and singer of comic songs, Harry Rickards, Henry Benjamin Leete, who also knew a thing or two about shouting things from rooftops and drumming up interest, for in March 1910, aged sixty-six, with little more than eighteen months of life left in him, Harry Rickards had been in the business for over fifty years, in fact he'd been in Australia thirty-nine years, having been born in Stratford, London, and travelled to Australia as an escape from his puritanical parents, and by the time he brought out Harry Houdini, Harry Rickards had well over five hundred people on his payroll, was attracting the greatest names in entertainment from all over the world to perform at numerous theatres around the country, often as part of his Tivoli Circuit, which took in Melbourne, Adelaide, Brisbane, Perth and many points between—including the Theatre Royal, aka the Olympia, in Coolgardie at the time that David Wynford Carnegie was breaking his back in those parts, and given the usual dearth of entertainment there, and the diggers' need for distraction from their relentless and often thankless pursuits, it is not inconceivable that Carnegie and his good friend Lord Percy Douglas took in a Harry Rickards performance one night in the late 1890s—and was known as the largest promotor of music hall acts in the world, and so, like Houdini, like Lord Northcliffe, Harry Rickards knew how to turn heads, which he did via an advertising campaign that made news of just how much he was paying to bring Houdini over from Europe—*At Enormous Expense!*—which in itself, as Rickards knew, was enough to get the punters excited. Indeed, this holy trinity of entertainers and advertisers did such a good job of promoting Houdini's record-breaking attempt that one could have been forgiven for thinking that the international daredevil would be limiting his Down Under stunts to those performed in his Voisin biplane, which of course was not the case at all—it was simply that aviation was, thanks to the efforts of showmen like Northcliffe, taking a firm hold of the public's imagination—for Houdini had booked theatres and other venues (Rickards would never have wasted such an opportunity) up and down the eastern seaboard of Australia, not the least of which occurred about a month before his Diggers Rest attempt, not in a theatre but on Melbourne's Queen's Bridge on Thursday 17 February at 1.30pm during a heatwave in which temperatures had soared to almost 40°C, a fact that no doubt troubled those in the twenty thousand-strong crowd in coats and hats lining the bridge and either bank of the Yarra, but one that didn't seem to bother Houdini at all, for he was dressed in bright blue bathers from neck to knee and smiling brightly as his aide, Franz Kukol, went about the business of cuffing his hands behind his back before wrapping him in heavy chains, once round the neck, once across the shoulders, twice around the torso and arms and once round the hips, closing off each end with a separate padlock, all the while Houdini smiled and chuckled with the audience, even going as far as saying to the crowd that it was all just a trick, an illusion, there was no magic involved in the slightest, in fact there was no such thing as magic, despite dearly wishing there was: there was just no proof!— perhaps this admission had something to do with his mindset when he arrived Down Under, his uncertainty regarding the future, the fact that he was starting to see through his own act and grow weary of it, a fact he made clear to the press a couple of months later in Sydney when he admitted to not really being interested in the handcuff act any longer, he wanted to explore other "mysteries," which is to suggest that the smiles that day on the Queen's Bridge, the pauses for effect, the nervous looks down from the parapet at the muddy waters below, were all part of the act, part of the illusion that now included not only his stunts but also the man himself—and so he went through the motions of repeating the handcuff routine one more time, hyping up the crowd, having independent audience members tug on the chains to show that the illusion was not in anything having been left loose or unlocked, waiting at the very edge of the parapet for the whooping and cheering to crescendo and at that very moment—master that he was he could feel when the time was just right, when the leap would take the crowd to even greater heights of excitement—jumping, which he did feet-first, the added weight of the chains and locks, some twelve kilograms, ensuring a rapid descent into the unexpectedly muddy riverbed—that part of the Yarra was barely more than ten feet deep at the time—where, shielded from view by the murk, he set about freeing himself, a task that took, according to the timekeepers, over two minutes, all the while the crowd waited nervously in silence and the police in their rowboats sat turning slowly on the weak current—one story has it that at this juncture, with everyone staring at the now smooth point where Houdini had entered the water, a black-clad figure moved through the crowd in the direction of one of Houdini's assistants and asked, "Are you connected with the chap who's just gone down?" and when the assistant, probably Franz Kukol, said that yes indeed he was, the dark figure handed him a card and whispered, "In case he shouldn't come up," before merging back into the crowd; later it would emerge that written on the card were the contact details of a local undertaker—meanwhile all twenty thousand spectators held their collective breath along with Houdini who was taking far longer than they thought survivable to free himself from those chains, all of a sudden everyone forgot about how hot it was, everyone was down there with him willing him up and beginning to feel the early reflections of shock, even the police started manoeuvring their boats towards the scene of his disappearance, perhaps this was the answer to his looming existential crisis, a dramatic way to exit the stage for good, I wonder if he thought about it while down there in the mud casually, almost resignedly, getting himself out of those bonds, maybe he could just stay down here and beat death to the punch, it would certainly do wonders for his own myth, the headlines would be bigger than ever, and he wouldn't have to endure all the soul searching of finding a new purpose, he could go out with the one thing he'd built his life around, the thing that was beginning to be threatened by a vastly and speedily changing cultural landscape, one that would have audiences turning to other mediums, other thrills, other mindsets, the explosion of cinema was imminent, vaudeville was becoming quaint, pretty soon defying death would hold only limited interest for people, the magic of which he was capable would pale in the face of the magic of cinema—film, like aviation, was taking off and if he didn't find the motivation to reinvent himself and embrace these mediums he might as well stay down there up to his armpits in the mud of the filthy Yarra, perhaps death could be his final trick, his last illusion, the symbol of a dying art snuffed out amid cheers from above. As the timekeeper registered that he had now been underwater for well over two minutes, Houdini emerged, one hand grasping the chains, the other raised in a triumphant fist—according to several versions of the story, Houdini was not the only one to come up from the riverbed that day, for it is claimed by some that on plunging into the mud he also dislodged a corpse that floated up beside him like a majestic grouper, shocking not only the bystanders but also the Master himself who had to be rescued and hauled aboard one of the police boats; such were the stories that followed him around, put about by any number of sources, no doubt Rickards and Northcliffe among them, for there are few official accounts to corroborate claims of an additional body in the water, and the even fewer photographs of the event that survive show only the Great Man bobbing in the Yarra, but to be fair these pictures are blurry at best and, like those supposed images of the Loch Ness

Monster, indecipherable at worst, so we cannot be certain, maybe it is true, will we ever know? It's bizarre to think that none of these stunts were ends-in-themselves but always a means to promoting something else, one result of which was the booklet published by the Aerial League of Australia and written by Lieutenant George Taylor, 'Wanted at Once! An Aerial Defence Fleet for Australia – A National Call to Australians,' a publication that included many images of Houdini in flight (as well as the good Lieutenant himself having a go) and warning about the increasing air preparedness and belligerence of Japan; it had the desired effect, for later that same year the Australian Minister of Defence, the Right Honourable Sir George Pearce—born in Adelaide in 1870, trained as a carpenter before moving to Coolgardie in 1893 to prospect for gold, and then, luckless, relocating to Perth where he went on to become a Senator for Western Australia and eventually Minister of Defence—travelled to Britain in order to inspect and learn about the advances the Motherland was making in aviation, a mission that, following serious talks with allied war men at the Brooklands Aerodrome, resulted in Sir George establishing an aviation program back in Australia, including the acquisition of four aircraft from the British Government as well as two British instructors who would help develop the skills and machinery that soon became the Australian Air Force; it was a fleet that would, as the Australian Flying Corps, go on to play a role in the Allied victory of World War I, fighting alongside the British in the Middle East in 1916 and, one year later, sending three squadrons to France, the third of which distinguished itself by delivering a significant blow to German morale when it aided in bringing down lauded enemy ace Manfred von Richthofen, aka the Red Baron, while the Second Squadron of the AFC continued bombing the Germans as they retreated along the Western Front, earning significant praise from one General Trenchard, commander of the Royal Flying Corps; and well-deserved it was, for among all the armies boasting an air corps, the AFC, with only one hundred and seventy-eight killed of 2,694 soldiers, sustained a much smaller casualty rate than most, and contributed greatly to crushing the Germans, the pride from which still flows in many an Australian's blood to this day in the form of the national reverence for the diggers of WWI, which is commemorated nationwide each year on 25 April, ANZAC Day, through the ceremonies of the Dawn Service. But before we start celebrating Harry Houdini as the catalyst for what would be a great Allied victory and the introduction of Australia into world politics, we must not forget that the whole business for him began on a German military parade ground just outside Hamburg in November 1909, in Wandsbek to be precise, where in exchange for use of the Hufaren parade grounds, the magician would, no doubt with the aid of his vastly more experienced mechanic Brassac, teach the German soldiers about his aircraft and the principles of flight—it is even suggested he gave them flying lessons—a fact he was keen to erase from public record and memory, putting it about that all of his flying took place in Australia, and burning up all the photographs that were taken of him posing with the Germans—all seemingly except one:

And so while Houdini's Australian tour unquestionably contributed to the push for the establishment of Australian and British air corps, and by extension an eventual Allied victory, thus impacting the course of the twentieth century, he also had a hand in introducing the Germans to flight—at which they would go on to excel in WWII—and it is perhaps therefore safer to say that he contributed greatly to the concept of aerial warfare in general, had a foot in both camps, as it were, the ethics of which is impossible to judge, and yet the end result is the same in that whatever Pandora's box he helped prise open, the fact is that his stunts contributed to the shaping of history with a rippling effect that would include, a few decades down the road, the Space Race, the Moon Landing, the International Space Station, satellite communication, the development of the internet and the mass and instantaneous transfer of information, the Challenger disaster, Apollo 13, 11 September 2001 and the disappearance of MH370. It's bizarre to think that, after leaving Australia, Harry Houdini would never fly again and his beloved Voisin would vanish without a trace, bizarre that flight was only a brief chapter in his miraculous life, being as it was an obsession that lasted barely a year, and his actual flying life lasting less than half that; how things can change so suddenly, so quickly, like when I returned home from the final tour of Cripp's Circus and visited my father and found him in a state of abject confusion, his house littered with pieces of paper stuck to objects marked "Refrigerator," "Telephone," "Bathroom," "Keys," "Photograph of Marigold (wife)," "Photograph of Travis (nurse)," and while I'd known he was not in the best of health when I'd left home for that tour, it was a shock to come back and see different coloured pieces of string running like firing synapses through his gloomy house, each labelled to signify the way towards a different area, "Kitchen," "Toilet," "Bedroom," "Front Door," "Back Door," like a sort of domestic flightpath between household destinations, a pattern once familiar now slipping from memory, the image of his wife going, going, going, receding into the fog, disappearing off the radar, the co-ordinates of a life to which he was clinging—wouldn't we all?—a final attempt, like Captain Zaharie Ahmad Shah and his waypoints to oblivion, like the dipping of the aircraft's nose towards the island of his birth, Penang, a desperate attempt to find some sort of order amid the disorder, to set it all out, to make it all make sense, to stand back and say, "Ah, well *that* makes sense!" in the end to gain a modicum of control over things that are by nature out of control and avoid spiralling off into the black unknown, the black unknowing, from which there is no coming back, no miraculous reappearing, no sleight of hand, these were unbreakable handcuffs, and so the old man traced those lines through the house, like that plane over the Andaman Sea, blind and unreachable, the old ringmaster who once commanded the attention of thousands, who introduced so many people to the world of the bizarre and unexpected and unexplainable, now himself being introduced to such a world by his failing faculties, a world in which everything had become bizarre, unexpected, unexplainable, a box of tissues, a bunch of bananas, a shoe; sometimes he would sit mesmerised by the most mundane thing, the cardboard roll at the end of the paper towel supply, marvelling at it, thinking it over, peering through it like a telescope, hooting into it like an owl, for hours—*hours*—only to repeat it again the next time we got to the end of the roll. I moved into his house immediately, primarily to take care of him but also to get out of the house I'd shared with my lost girls, that ghost house in which I kept finding Alison's long blonde hairs that hissed like taipans on the furniture; the few people to whom I spoke about my plan to become my father's carer, including Vasily, suggested that it was a good idea; you have to stay afloat; you have to move forward; helping your father will help you; there was no end to their goodwill and kind words; a change of scenery will do you good; a new chapter of your life; and all of the things they said were right, it did help me to care for Dad, and though I didn't tell anyone about it, my new focus on the Voisin helped too; whenever I was not with Dad, I was out at Tullamarine with Southy in his workshop, sitting in the aircraft as it slowly came together, learning the language, learning the controls, "pedal," "rudder," "steering wheel," "choke," "revolutions per minute," "roll," "bank," I muttered them to myself as I handled each part, learning the lexicon of flight, the language of that faraway world, the language also of Captain Zaharie, and imagined manoeuvring the plane at altitude, guiding it left and right, looking at the small crowd below waving hands and hats up at me, bringing it down with a bump onto the rough surface of the old Plumpton paddock and ushering in a new age, and the deeper I dove into the events surrounding Houdini's flight, the less time and capacity I had to investigate the disappearance of MH370, or at least the less preoccupied with it I became, for I was now filling myself up with history down to the finest detail, pouring in the past, while externally I dressed myself in it, now wearing the coats, shoes and hats of the time, immersing myself fully in the role. I was also, as the months went by, filling myself up with details about my father's condition and, more importantly, its treatment, or rather management, given that there is to date no cure or even reliable and effective medication for the disease named in July 1910—mere months after Houdini's fateful flight—after one Aloysius 'Alois' Alzheimer, psychiatrist, neuropathologist and prolific cigar-smoker, in Emil Kraepelin's *Textbook of Psychiatry (8th ed.)*, which he (Kraepelin) described as *presenility* after noting the results of an incredibly detailed, almost obsessive study conducted by his colleague and friend Alois on a woman in her early fifties named Auguste Deter, born Johanna Auguste Caroline Hochmann, who was referred to Alzheimer's care by her family after displaying unusual and acute feelings of jealousy towards her husband together with memory loss and temporary vegetative states, all of which manifested in her being unable to find her way about her house, dragging her bedsheets from one room to the next, hiding objects, while also convinced that someone was trying to kill her and screaming incessantly; her husband, Carl August Wilhelm Deter, a railway worker, was unable to treat her at home and so she was admitted, in November 1901, to the Institution for the Mentally Ill and for Epileptics in Frankfurt (aka *Irrenschloss*, "Castle of the Insane") where she came under the care of Alois who spoke with  her at length regarding her jealousy and her suspicions towards her husband—incidentally, Alzheimer was a close friend and colleague of the neurologist Wilhelm Erb who once, while on a scientific expedition in Algeria, contacted Alois with an urgent request for expertise when his travelling companion, banking magnate Otto Geisenheimer, suffered a crisis of GPI (general paralysis of the insane, of which Alois was a noted expert) and required the best attention money could buy; without a moment to spare, Alzheimer had dashed off to Africa but was unfortunately too late to intervene in Geisenheimer's fate, for the man died forthwith, and the trip might have been in vain had it not been for Geisenheimer's widow Cecilia who, not three weeks after her husband's demise, asked Alzheimer to marry her, which he did, and over the next seven years the pair had three children until, in 1901, Cecilia Geisenheimer, now Alzheimer, died during the birth of their third child Maria, thus precipitating a period of grief which was only getting started when Auguste Deter was delivered into Alois' care—and not only did he ask her about her husband Carl and his supposed infidelities but he asked her many, many things in order to understand her more fully, the following being from a transcript of one of their sessions:

Alzheimer: What is your name?
Deter: Auguste.
A: Family name?
D: Auguste.
A: What is your husband's name?
D: (*hesitates, finally answers*) I believe... Auguste.
A: Your husband?
D: Oh, no no no.
A: How old are you?
D: Fifty-one.
A: Where do you live?
D: Oh, you have been to our place.
A: Are you married?
D: Oh, I am so confused.
A: Where are you right now?
D: Here and everywhere, here and now. You must not think badly of me.
A: Where are you at the moment?
D: We will live there.
A: Where is your bed?
D: Where should it be?

Around midday, Frau Auguste D. ate pork and cauliflower.

A: What are you eating?
D: Spinach. (*She was chewing meat.*)
A: What are you eating now?
D: First I eat potatoes and then horseradish.
A: Write a "5."

She writes: "A woman."

A: Write an "8."

She writes: "Auguste." (While she is writing she says, "I have lost myself.")

This last was something Auguste Deter repeated over and again: "I have lost myself" (*Ich habe mich verloren*), sometimes screaming it and disturbing everyone on the ward, other times sitting alone muttering to herself, which suggests, like a plane crash unfolding slowly, that she was aware of her degenerating mind, there was a part of her that understood that she was in a downward spiral, a process in which the waypoints of her life were disappearing one after the other, and I imagine Alois Alzheimer in his own grief, having lost his wife mere months beforehand, speaking to his patient, asking her soft questions and taking copious notes, listening to her hesitant voice and transcribing her words as she said them, "*Ich habe mich verloren*," "*Ich habe mich verloren*," and observing as her demented state worsened, bizarre really, because she was so young, barely into her fifties, when she should have retained full use of her capacities, been in full command of herself, and this was what attracted Alois to the case, for he'd seen this sort of thing a few times before, but never in someone as young as Auguste, it usually occurred in people approaching their eighties, astonishing, she now displayed no awareness of time or space, displayed barely any evidence of active memory, everything was gone or at least jumbled around, mixed up, misplaced, chaos, and I wonder if Alois, at some level, even for just a minute, wished he could have joined her there in complete oblivion, in that condition which he called at the time—it would be a while before the term Alzheimer's Disease emerged, but Auguste would be the first person diagnosed with it, albeit retroactively—the "Disease of Forgetfulness." Following

Auguste's death in 1906, Dr. Alzheimer requested that her medical file and brain be sent to him in Munich where he'd taken up a position at his good friend Emil Kraepelin's laboratory in the Royal Psychiatric Hospital at which he could continue his studies of senile illnesses and receive cadavers for examination, a burgeoning field in which he was a pioneer, a major milestone of his career being his investigation of the Deter brain which revealed senile plaques and neurofibrillary tangles, the signs of what we now know as Alzheimer's Disease, findings he would deliver via a lecture later that same year at the Tübingen meeting of the Southwest German Psychiatrists, which did not go over as planned, for the audience was preoccupied with hearing the paper that followed his on "compulsive masturbation," and thus he left the stage to thin applause and attracted zero questions or comments; nevertheless, laboratory studies of the life and death of the brain had well and truly begun, as had studies in another field that would soon dovetail with the one inaugurated by Alzheimer, namely the field of transhumanism, the ideas inherent to which were first presented by one J.B.S. Haldane FRS—nephew of British Secretary of State for War, Richard Burdon Haldane, 1st Viscount Haldane, friend to media baron and owner of the *Daily Mail* and the *Daily Mirror* Lord Northcliffe, 1st Viscount Northcliffe, who in turn was a good friend of Harry Houdini's—J.B.S., aka John Burdon Sanderson, aka 'Jack,' in stark contrast to his uncle's sluggishness when it came to embracing new technologies in the field of aviation, was the first to coin the terms "clone" and "cloning" in biology, as well as "ectogenesis," the former two of which he introduced to the world in his 1963 paper 'Biological Possibilities for the Human Species of the Next Ten Thousand Years,' where he outlined the notion of using genetics to engineer superior human beings; but it was an earlier work, *Daedalus; or, Science and the Future*, published in the UK in 1924, in which Haldane—curiously, in 1923, Houdini would produce, direct and star in the silent film *Haldane of the Secret Service*, one of the few movies made by the failed Houdini Picture Corporation, and one that met with few accolades and even fewer profits—laid the foundations of transhumanist thought and proclaimed: "The chemical or physical inventor is always a Prometheus. There is no great invention, from fire to flying, which has not been hailed as an insult to some god. But if every physical and chemical invention is a blasphemy, every biological invention is a perversion. There is hardly one which, on first being brought to the notice of an observer from any nation which had not previously heard of their existence, would not appear to him as indecent and unnatural," and going on to envision a future in which humans were responsible for their own evolution via the use of advanced and advancing technologies to control the way our bodies adapted and functioned in meeting the demands of the contemporary world as well as the challenges posed by disease and ageing, concluding on an upbeat note: "I am optimistic about the future. Science can make us fly and live in space in future, perhaps in the next century, like our mythological epics have Gods flying in the sky." As the century marched on, others picked up on Haldane's ideas, English evolutionary biologist Julian Huxley pop-ularising the term "transhuman" by using it for the title of an influential paper in 1957 in which he discussed the probability of the human race transcending itself through bionic implants and cognitive enhancements, while in 1960 the Japanese metabolist architect Noboru Kawazoe wrote of the "rapid progress of comm-unication technology" giving rise to the implantation of a "brain wave receiver" in the human population, a development that would allow the wearer to receive the thoughts of all around them and transmit their own thoughts to others resulting in the annihilation of individual consciousness and the rise of the singular will of humankind as a whole; but it was in 1966 that transhumanism really gathered a head of steam when Iranian-American Fereidoun

M. Esfandiary—who would go on to change his name to FM-2030, more on this shortly—futurist, author, teacher, philosopher, athlete and incurable optimist, started identifying people using technology to move from a human to a posthuman state as "transhuman," therefore fostering a transhumanist movement that had its active origins in the early 1980s in Los Angeles at the University of California where Esfandiary, now FM-2030, was teaching courses on his Third Way. Born in 1930 in Brussels, Belgium, his father was an Iranian diplomat which meant that FM-2030 and his family were always on the move—he claimed to have lived in seventeen differ-ent countries by the time he was eleven—he was handsome and athletic, representing Iran in basketball at the 1948 Olympics in London, an experience that had a profound impact on him, for it was there that he began to see right through the entire concept of winning, of being *first*, the whole idea of competition, prizes and awards he saw as a detriment to humankind, the thirst for victory being merely a remnant of a disposition we no longer needed, an attitude that was stifling our evolution as a species; he favoured a gentler, more inclusive approach to life, arguing that we would strive to make advances without cutthroat competition, without the demands of business, an attitude that extended to his vegetarian diet, stating that he'd never eat anything that had a mother; he never married, saying he did not believe in the bonds of marriage and that one person should never own another, though he did have a partner for the last thirty years of his life, Flora Schnall, and in the mid-1970s he legally changed his name from Fereidoun M. Esfandiary to FM-2030 on the grounds that, firstly, he hoped to live until 2030 which would be his hundredth birthday, secondly, he viewed standard naming conventions as reflecting ancient and outdated forms of thought that, again, were grounded in our former tribal existence and worked to limit the scope of our identities, forcing onto us concepts of gender, nationality, marital status and even economic status, and thirdly, being ever the optimist, he explained: "The name 2030 reflects my conviction that the years around 2030 will be a magical time. In 2030 we will be ageless and everyone will have an excellent chance to live forever. 2030 is a dream and a goal." It was difficult for me not to get caught up in his hopefulness, and I soon found myself digging up everything I could about him, reading as many of his writings as I could get my hands on, from his fictional works *The Day of Sacrifice*, *The Beggar*, and *Identity Card*, to his later philosophical treatises *Optimism One: The Emerging Radicalism*, *Telespheres*, *Are You a Transhuman?: Monitoring and Stimulating Your Personal Rate of Growth in a Rapidly Changing World*, and *Up-Wingers*, the latter being a very short but powerful work describing a new paradigm of non-binary thought that differentiated itself from the outdated political left-wing/right-wing model and claimed that society's natural inclination towards pessimism emerged from this kind of flat, horizontal thinking, and that no-one, regardless of their current leanings, would be able to affect any sort of meaningful change unless global society abandoned this left/right, right/wrong, winner/loser way of organising life and embraced the up-wing, which allows for change and fluidity and an end to, or at least a dramatic decrease in, suffering via all the advances in technology, in particular a mastery over death, but also including perfecting the human form and correcting its weaknesses and malfunctions. Part shaman, part showman, FM-2030 became the face of the transhumanist, up-wing movement appearing in magazines and newspapers, writing books and articles, teaching at universities, undertaking exhausting public speaking schedules, consulting to big business and generally positioning himself as the figurehead of a glorious future in which technology would be capable of harnessing the power of the sun, improving our quality of life, providing an abundance of sustenance and companionship and even, and this was at the heart of his philosophy, bringing us immortality, which he illustrated eloquently (he seemed always measured, direct and erudite) with his knowingly rolling Persian accent during an appearance on the *Larry King Live* show in 1989 in promotion of his book *Are You a Transhuman?*:

Larry: We're going to live longer, aren't we?

FM-2030: If you're around in the year 2010, there's a very, very good chance that you'll be around in the year 2030. If you're around in 2030, there's an excellent chance that you can coast to immortality. Indefinite life-spans. Mind you, Larry, not with these bodies and certainly not on this planet only!

He anticipated a cashless society and one in which you would carry a communication device with you everywhere so you could conduct business wherever you were, at the beach or by the pool; he also envisaged a global society in which racism and other prejudices would fall by the wayside as our skin tones homogenised, international borders came to mean less and less, and rapid travel became possible via hypersonic space planes, as well as the growth of a centralised, computerised government as traditional forms of government eroded; here he is again on *Larry King*: "Some of the greatest changes in this country of the last twenty-five years—the women's movement, the civil rights movement, the consumer movement, the environmental movement, the youth movement, the sexual revolution, etc., etc.—all these were spearheaded by people outside government, and it's interesting that most of the administrations... were able to do very little to stop them," all of which is to say that he was a radical, a revolutionary, a prophet, and his prophecies were all based on an optimism generated by a faith in technology and progress, which is to say that I took to him immediately, and it is one of life's cruelties that I did not have the chance to meet him, for he died thirty years short of his mark, in 2000, of pancreatic cancer—I will, however, refrain from saying that I'll *never* meet FM-2030, for upon his death he was placed in cryonic suspension at the Alcor Life Extension Foundation in Scottsdale, Arizona, where his body remains to this day, so there's always hope—something that, I think, FM-2030 would have agreed with: there is always hope! Central to his beliefs was the use of technology to improve our lives and treat disease and bodily malfunction, in terms of both prolonging life indefinitely and improving the quality of that life, which was how I came to learn about him, researching as I was the various methods and theories regarding the treatment of my father's worsening condition—I'm a firm believer in the notion that everything and everyone comes to you at the right time; I've had little choice but to believe in the powers of fate, the alternative is unbearable—for as my Voisin replica came together in Southy's workshop in Tullamarine, my father's mind was coming apart; it was now taking much longer for him to recognise me and understand where I fit into his life, and when at last he did his expression would soften, his eyes would sparkle and he'd nod knowingly as though he was not remembering me, *per se*, but rather a nice story someone once told him; and if he attempted to roam anywhere within his house, despite the notes, despite the waypoints, despite the coloured pieces of string mapping his intended flightpaths, I would find him off-course, wandering in and out of the same room seemingly having just remembered something that was located wherever he *wasn't* and if I didn't intervene he would keep returning over and over, in and out of the same room, *ad infinitum*. He will need care, full-time care, very soon, but that sort of thing is expensive and ever since the closure of our family business there has been little money even for the most necessary things; nevertheless, I continue with my work, my research, for it gives me hope and despite everything I do feel positive about the future, just as FM-2030 would have encouraged me to feel, just as FM-2030 himself felt, I do feel that change is coming, change for the better, and we will move into a time in which we are not sceptical towards technology, in which we will view technology and nature as complementary, even as a single phenomenon, technology *as* nature, in which the organic and the synthetic will merge and human beings will play a central role in their own evolution and the evolution of our planet, that it is our fate to *become* fate and enter an age of abundance, not indulgence, but a time of plenty for all in which the old dynamics of left/right, have/have not, the old cronies that maintain scarcity in order to protect their own abundance, that dig up all the gold and tuck it away for themselves, all of it will soon come to be seen as wrong-headed and detrimental to everyone, not just those who miss out, not just the losers in this game, but detrimental even to the cronies themselves—case in point: Arthur Wellesley Bayley, the prospector who discovered what would come to be known as Bayley's Reward goldmine at Fly Flat in September 1892, one of the world's richest patches of land ever found, would die four years later of congestion of the lungs as a result of his exploits, a fate that was not uncommon at the time, respiratory illnesses accounting for many a digger's ultimate rest— a time in which scarcity itself will seem antiquated and pointless and *homo sapiens* will view life from an entirely new perspective, with an entirely new brain, the advances are already being made. Perhaps the most promising, so I discovered, is the rise of brain-computer interfaces using neural-lace technology, a process by which tiny electrodes are implanted into the brain tissue (or applied externally via a skullcap) for the purposes of improving brain function and facilitating things like memory and motor skills for people suffering brain injuries or disease, technology pushed by several companies, the more notable being Neuralink founded by one Elon Musk—who incidentally also owns a company called SpaceX which sent up Demo-2, the first space mission launched by a private company, and the first private company to dock with the International Space Station, not to mention arm-wrestling Richard Branson and Jeff Bezos on who will be the first to send civilians into space—whose current focus is treating the infirm via an implanted computer which mimics the function of the biological hippocampus in terms of both input and output, ie. serving as a memory prosthesis, retaining and co-ordinating information that means the patient can scrunch up all those labels placed around the house and roll up those pieces of string leading this way and that; for now, for us, this treatment is cutting edge and too expensive, but I'm hopeful of it soon entering the mainstream; for the people at Neuralink, however, this is just the beginning, for it is envisaged that this technology will help not only those with brain damage and illness but healthy people as well, that these implants will boost memory, cognitive performance and overall knowledge, all of which would be delivered to the subject via computer using a process called "mind-uploading," "mind transfer," or "whole brain emulation," which is to be achieved by scanning or mapping the subject's brain, including long-term memory, and then transferring this information to a computer or other device which then, in theory, behaves in precisely the same manner as the human subject; where it gets interesting (if one isn't interested already!) is when the reverse is performed, when information stored in a computing system is downloaded to chips embedded in the subject's brain tissue, a map of the mind imported into, or superimposed onto, the human subject, in the case of someone with Alzheimer's replicating what was there before—some take an overly precious, holier than thou approach to consciousness, but scientists have proven that what we know as thoughts, patterns, processes, a sense of humour, anything that contributes to our overall persona, is pure science, all eminently traceable, observable and, importantly for us, replicable, and therefore not, as many believe, some nebulous, ineffable, God-given magic; there is no magic, only craft, only logic (the Handcuff King was more scientist than magician)—all of which poses great opportunities for the human race, not just in terms of managing physical illness but also in terms of the quest for immortality, for if we are in agreement that our consciousness is the core of our identity—and it appears we are; was my good friend and plane-builder Southy any less himself on account of his prosthetic leg?—then all we need do is transfer the computer-generated replica of our mental and emotional processes into another vehicle, whether that's another flesh-and-blood body or indeed some sort of auto-maton, just as they do in the film *Avatar*, in order to eschew the principles of cell decay (which is proving a much tougher nut to crack) and live on for eternity. Couple this with the tracking, surveil-lance, and data-storage technology we have already, and you get the possibility of being able to animate a being—either organic (a human body) or synthetic (a robot)—with the stored information of any one particular consciousness, which is to say that we are not far off being able to bring people back from the dead, the loved ones we've lost, and thus to banish the concept of loss to the past and seize for ourselves the controls of fate. As my research continued, and I vanished for days and weeks down this rabbit hole and that, tearing myself away only to care for my father and visit Southy's hangar at Tullamarine in order to keep abreast of the elements of the Voisin's construction, I learned of another extremely exciting development on what is known as the "intelligence amplification" front, one that would change and amplify my hopes for the future and our chances of learning the fate of MH370; while all the above was wonderful news for keeping us alive and healthy *as we are*, if we could have bionics that helped improve our daily lives—á la Southy—it was entirely feasible, given the emerging technology, that we could utilise these implants to enhance our cognitive abilities, which is to say that rather than functioning as a replica of the mind this technology would improve the performance of any given mind via a brain-computer interface which could, in theory, connect your brain to the internet as well as any and all data storage devices and facilities, and that would mean access to untold information, a super-brain capable of infinite knowledge, an unending feed of facts, ideas and stories that would be the crowning glory of all the technological developments made throughout the twentieth century, one that could launch us headlong into the future armed with every ounce of knowledge ever generated by the human race; undoubtedly the ethics will be a nightmare, but at the end of the day humans would need to decide what they want for themselves, for everything has risks, imagine the bravery of those first pilots climbing aboard those machines that were basically box-kites fitted with eighty-horsepower engines, and taking them up to three thousand feet with nothing but a cap turned backwards and a pair of goggles for safety; think of those doomed Challenger astronauts reaching out to "touch the face of God," their optimism as they walked across the bridge to climb into their shuttle; imagine having all the information in history, every image, every telephone record, every flightpath not only stored beneath our soil, but accessible to us by mere thought, no more mysteries, no more guesswork, a pure coalescence of biology and technology that would turn us into all-knowing, all-seeing entities; it would be the end of wars, of prejudice, of all sorts of binary thought processes that lead to suffering. What's more, we would know the fate of *that flight*, for without question the information is there somewhere, maybe not on some government server or document, maybe they in fact do not know and there is no cover-up—despite the evidence suggesting huge corruption, or at least strategic silence on the part of the Malaysian government, for admitting that Captain Zaharie Shah was responsible opens them up to all sorts of criticisms—but I *am* certain there is a particular combination of facts—weather patterns, ocean currents, winds, wear rates on aircraft parts, responses to trauma, instances of adultery in the relationships of pilots, radio waves, satellite imagery, radicalisation, UFOs, ocean birds, whale song frequencies, the Nasdaq—a certain combination of seemingly un-related data that will tell us exactly what transpired that night somewhere over the Indian Ocean, which we will one day figure out via cognitive processes enabled by technological advances. The more I read about it the more sure I became, the more comfort I took in the rise of technology and its infiltration into our lives and bodies—in fact, to say I took comfort is slightly misleading, for the more I learned the more anxious I was for these technologies to come to fruition, for the future to arrive more quickly than it appeared to be doing, for the days to go faster, for results to be published sooner, and the more I read, the more I wanted to read, to douse myself in information, to be engulfed by it, to wallow and roll around in it like a traveller washed up on his native shores might scoop up handfuls of wet sand and smear it about his face; my hope took me deeper and fuelled my optimism, which in turn spurred me on to go deeper in order to learn and absorb as much as I could, all the while the Voisin replica was taking shape; within six months, Southy had managed to source nearly all of the required materials—minus the Belgian linen, delivery of which we were still waiting for—thanks to the designs we'd procured from the Australian Vintage Aviation Society, which not only furnished us with three-view drawings but was also instrumental in locating the desired parts and materials so that by the end of that first year my chipper friend had measured and cut and checked and double-checked all the necessary elements of the main fuselage section, which came together in good time that summer; I'd hoped we'd be able to have the machine ready for 18 March of the coming year, but as the end of summer drew near (and we were still waiting for

the bloody linen), that target seemed at first unlikely then impossible as it whizzed by and we were forced to wait another full year,
which at first I took as a disappointment but then ultimately embraced, for it allowed us time to get things right (and to receive the
bloody linen)—plus, while Southy was enthusiastic and dedicated
to the project, he was hampered by his disability, which meant he
required a lot more energy to perform many tasks than he otherwise
would, so the fact that we had another full year—I was determined
to make the flight on 18 March—meant that he didn't have to bust
his guts to get the thing built. By the middle of 2019 the fuselage
was together—also by then my father's condition had somewhat
stabilised thanks to the medications the specialist had him on; I was
warned, however, that this levelling out would only be temporary,
for the trajectory of any sort of dementia is downwards at a variety
of inclines, and so I continued my research, reaching out to university departments to put my father forward for treatments featuring the latest advances in neurotechnology, for the more I read the
more sure I was that we were on the brink of a huge breakthrough
in the field; the technology was there, the knowledge was there, the
ethics were catching up, but of course it was all still outrageously
expensive and the only way to receive this sort of treatment was
to be involved in its development, which without question had its
risks, and I was not blind to them, so it was a matter of lesser evils:
would the treatment make him suffer more than he already was?
also, knowing my father, Arthur Bernard Cripp, ringmaster, lion-
tamer, crowd-pleaser, it was not his style to wither away, I knew
for certain he'd want to try almost anything, especially if it seemed
off the wall, the more outrageous the better, and so I had few qualms
in reaching out to various research centres to gauge their interest
in taking on Dad's case. I was becoming excited by a new and highly
advanced form of intervention involving an implant placed inside
the brain's blood vessels, a procedure that could be performed as

day surgery and did not require any risky open-brain operations, being trialled at a university in Melbourne and funded by an Australian neuro-technology corporation—I couldn't believe our luck—I called the clinic immediately and again luck was on our side, we were invited to come in to the Defries Institute of Neuroscience and Mental Health for an interview conducted by one Prof. Devlyn Broadbent, whose small, thin and tanned marathon-runner stature stood in stark contrast to her obviously large intellect, sensitivity and effervescent personality, a personality that changed down several gears when she dived into the interview:

Broadbent: What is your name?
Dad: Bernard.
B: That is your middle name. What is your first?
D: Um. Oh bugger.
B: What colour is my shirt?
D: Red and white. (*It was yellow.*)
B: What does that word say on the wall over there?
D: Quickly. (*It said 'spade.'*)
B: How many fingers am I holding up?
D: Window?
B: What is your son's name?
D: Bernard. (*That was a trick question, but Prof. Broadbent did not realise it. Either that, or it was a trick answer.*)
B: What is your name?
D: Do you know, my dear, I know it but I just can't say it. I'm ah, I'm a bit lost... *Marigold!*

I explained to Prof. Broadbent—who was initially distracted by my antiquated attire before telling me that she liked my hat—that Marigold was his wife, my mother, whom we'd lost many years before, and as she placed a steady hand on my father's and told him he was doing really well in a way that was not condescending and gave him the dignity he deserved, it occurred to me that she was the first woman I'd spent time with in about two, almost three, years—the nurses who came to our home were men—not by design but just due to the forces that were at play in my life at the time, I'd forgotten how calming and grounding it could be to be in the presence of women, and I dearly hoped that, although he wouldn't have been able to articulate it to himself, Dad had felt the same. Our interviewer then repeated her questions, though this time she gave him the answers beforehand; still, while the answers differed from the first round they were no closer to being correct, which she would later tell me was good for the study, for the proposed implant would hopefully help him to retain information and bolster his short-term memory, which in the following months it did—the implant was a success, not a complete cure but enough to spur a vast improvement in short-term memory and information reten- tion—just as I believed it would, the only problem being that when they removed the implant, as was required following the comple- tion of the eight-week trial, my father's mind went back to its old tricks, and when I asked Prof. Broadbent if we couldn't simply leave the implant where it was, I was told that there were still eth- ical concerns and that they didn't yet have approval to use it perm- anently. And so while the removal of the implant was disappoint- ing, the trial itself was heartening, though it seemed that after the removal my father's condition was worse than before, or perhaps it just seemed so given the general improvement over the preceding months; either way, as the summer drew near, our house again became a land of shadows and sighs, the notes went back up on the walls, furniture and appliances, but were more or less useless, and if I'm completely honest I was often relieved to be able to take the drive up the highway to Southy's workshop to inspect his progress and continue practicing manoeuvres now that the fuselage had been completed as well as the tailplane and rudder, the front elevators and undercarriages (all three of them: nose, tail and main), the wings (we'd at last received the linen) and control systems; it was all together and looking magnificent; seeing it up close was like a dream, or rather as though a dream had leapt from my mind into the physical world, the fact I could touch it, sit in it, manipulate the controls, just as the Great Harry Houdini had done in the early days of aviation, made my body tingle, I could feel the thrill he felt over a century before, the wonder, the sense that something miraculous was in the offing, that we were on the brink of something, something life-changing, Earth-changing, something that would divert the course of human history and define centuries to come, I felt it in the steering wheel, the hope, the promise, the optimism, what this flight would herald, the excitement and fear of the pioneer (Houdini would later admit that his hands were trembling as he climbed into his Voisin for the attempt at the Australian record), for there were, and are, always risks, there's always the chance that you'll never come back, that you'll be lost, that your attempt will fail, that as much as you try to stage-manage it, despite all the safety measures and protocols you put in place, things can go wrong and all the hope and optimism in the world can send you spiralling off into darkness, the poison-dart of fate; that fear is always there, was always there, and if there's anything constant in a world of change and progress it is the fear, the fear of loss, of becoming lost, for nothing worth having comes without risk, to wit: the risk of losing what you already have, and it is frightening because with progress, with change, there will inevitably be losses, loss comes bundled up in the very definition of change, and sitting at the controls of that Voisin II replica on those stifling summer afternoons, I felt not only the excitement of what lay just over the horizon, what unknown treasures were to be found in the skies, but also the feeling that

Harry Houdini carried with him on the steamer out to the Great Southern Land that he had lost or was in the process of losing something, that reinvention was required but maybe he was too wounded and tired to undergo yet another reinvention, at only thirty-six he had become old, as had Zaharie at fifty-two, and at only forty-four I too felt the weight of the years, the scars on my hands and face from a life on fire, I too was, if I let myself think about it, which I tried so hard not to, unsure of what to do or where to go next, after this stunt, after we packed away the aircraft for good, what then? after my father goes, what then? I had spent my life in a circus, what new avenues could possibly be open to me half-melted and broken? no, I did my best to ignore it, just as Houdini had done—I wonder if, when remaining on the muddy river-bed of the Yarra for effect, holding his breath for well over two minutes, having removed his manacles in the first forty-five seconds, waiting in the dark silence of those murky currents tossing his hair about, hearing the muffled cheers above, I wonder if these thoughts came to him then, while the crowd became increasingly agitated and the police started to peer over the sides of their boats and the mysterious shadowy undertaker slipped Franz Kukol his business card, whether Houdini, Erik Weisz, Ehrich Weiss, the Hungarian-born American citizen of the world, felt that there was now nothing else for him, or at least questioned what was out there, what was the use in coming up? what was the use in landing that plane (if he'd in fact ever get up there, damn winds)? I wonder too if Zaharie Shah had asked himself these questions, What now?, after life had ebbed away, after all the stories he'd told himself, after everything that had anchored him to life, each waypoint, had suddenly disappeared leaving him wandering like a ghost through his own home on the outskirts of Kuala Lumpur, from room to empty room, not knowing how or why he was there, merely arriving in one room—say, the former bedroom of one of his children, or even the bedroom he used to share with his wife, now so unlived-in, or the room where he sometimes watched movies on the big projection screen—just so he could sigh and move on to the next room in that house of sighs, and when he'd visited each of those echoing rooms, decked out in little but absence, tiny reminders of what used to be, and found nothing but ghosts, found himself absolutely and resoundingly alone, he'd settle into the comfortable and comforting chair of his simulator, three huge screens in front of him occupying almost his entire field of vision—so immersive, in such high definition as to feel almost real—selecting a flight path, maybe one he hadn't tried before in all his hours in his beloved sim, in all his 18,423 hours of actual flying experience, an origin and a destination that were completely new to him, uncharted territory, which would of course have the desired effect of occupying his mind, a healthy distraction from the anguish that had become the centre of his existence, the desolation that had crept in and was threatening to take over, to consume him completely, and the only thing he could think to do was to try to outrun it and fill the void with colour and movement, from city to city to city, over every ocean, waypoint to waypoint to waypoint, even random ones, waypoints he had to plug in manually because they were so off the beaten track as not to be listed in the software's defaults, along the Malacca Strait out over the Andaman Sea, down to the southern Indian Ocean, the middle of nowhere, impossible journeys, just to keep moving, that was key, to stay mobile, aloft, to overlay the absence of existential direction with the more immediate and tangible demands of geographical direction, the beginning, middle and end of the journey, they were laid out in front of him, they were real, he could look at them, plot them, they had meaning. But, of course, one can only run for so long, the tank soon runs dry, the immersive experience of the unknown can only distract for a while until one becomes familiar with it, the up and down, the away and the return, the beginning and the middle and the end; regardless of where he went, these journeys were always the same and once again he would find himself back in those empty rooms, with little but sighs for company, back in that simulator built for one with only the idea of skies for company, the idea of journeys, the idea of clouds, and the emptiness now dogged him even there in the place that was once his refuge, his Arcadia, that was once *him*, the absence followed him out, the distraction, like a drug, was no longer enough, it could never, if he was honest with himself, be enough, it would always fall short, the relief only ever temporary, and so where it once evaporated whenever he settled into the cockpit it came to find him even there because he knew, at heart, there would always be the return, the round trip, and the only way out of it was the linear journey, the one that is only ever away to never return; that, in the end, was the solution, the random chaotic journey that made no sense, that conformed to no pattern, not even to the pattern of the short history of pilot suicides, uncharted territory, *terra nullius*, the only journey left; I too felt a pit of grief that needed filling, that blind tunnel that ran right through him, a miasmic anguish clouding not only the dreamer but the entire dream, I too have known such anguish, and sitting there at the controls, imagining myself taking off and swooping about overhead, I felt the excitement and the fear coalesce into an eagerness to get going, to make the magic happen, and a desire for it to last *ad infinitum*, for the stunt to never stop, for the ultimate linear journey. The final major element to be fitted to the Voisin was the French E.N.V. motor, a rare specimen these days, the manufacturer having gone out of the engine-building business not long after Houdini went up at Diggers Rest, but thanks to the efforts of Ron and Rachel Voss of the Australian Vintage Aviation Society we were put in touch with an Austrian, one Sebastian Wlassak, collector, recluse, avoider of telephone calls, reluctant speaker of English (despite doing it very well), who owned some land about an hour southeast of Salzburg in a place called Imlau (near Werfen where, incidentally, much of *The Sound of Music* was filmed) and possessed, in one of his barns, all sorts of old aviation parts and memorabilia from the WWI period; as luck would have it, Wlassak (who I assumed would be quite old but was barely into his forties) did indeed possess an E.N.V. Type C engine, not quite in working order but nothing that we couldn't have fixed and serviced when it arrived in Melbourne, so Wlassak told me when at last I managed to get him on the phone, and then, despite his initial reluctance both to speak and to speak English, he went on at great length to tell me all sorts of things about himself including the fact that he'd moved to Imlau from Salzburg on account of "nerves" and had chosen his current locale because of the abundance of opportunities to "take the waters" at the various "Bads" scattered about the area, which was more or less the only reason he left the house other than to visit nearby Werfen for supplies, otherwise he spent all of his time building, dismantling and rebuilding things, mostly motorised machines, cars, motorcycles, tractors and, of course, old aircraft— I found, once he got going, Wlassak had a sort of Swissness about him, a smiling buoyancy and general cheer beneath the curmudgeonly exterior, which it seemed was not so much curmudgeonly as being unused to speaking with people—which he then sold to enthusiasts around the world and was how, so he said, he made his living, and yes he was happy to sell me the old E.N.V. engine he had, but it wasn't in working order and would need parts either sourced from another vintage collector or made up especially; rather than leaving this process in the hands of the Austrian, for I was always mindful of the looming 18 March deadline, I asked him to ship the motor as it was and I'd sort out the rest from my end, which he was happy (and "between you and me") relieved to do as that sort of restoration work would be "nothing short of a headache," for there was a limit to the patience, he told me, even of the solitary, even of those with little on their hands but time, and I told him I knew exactly what he meant. The motor was the last major component to arrive, which it did in November before going straight into "the garage" as Southy called it (but pronounced "garridge"), where, in late January, after much machining and head-scratching, it was delivered to our Tullamarine workshop wrapped in plastic as though it had just rolled off the assembly line, which meant that my brother in arms, Francis Southermore—who had become as obsessed with the project as I was (more or less), much to my satisfaction and relief, for in order to play a convincing Brassac one had to think of the Voisin as one's own flesh and blood—which meant that Southy had just over a month to fit the E.N.V. into the aircraft and have it ready to roll, a reasonable timeline it seemed, but one that turned out to run right up to the wire, with Southy pulling a few all-nighters in order to ensure that we made the date. When at last, after almost two years in construction, our Voisin II biplane was ready, we wheeled it out of the workshop and into the driveway that ran between the two long lines of attached storage sheds, its wingspan accommodated by the merest of margins, which meant that as we manoeuvred it into position Southy was directing my movements via a barrage of shouted orders interspersed with a thousand repetitions of "Careful! Careful! Careful!" as though a single bump would cause the thing to burst into flames—in the latter stages of completion, he seemed to forget that our mission was just as important to me as it was to him!—obviously we couldn't conduct a test flight here, but our aim in rolling it out there was to test the engine now that it had been mounted and the propeller fitted; it also gave me my first taste of being in the cockpit of the completed machine, which meant that all the controls were alive and I could start to get a feel for how the aircraft responded to my input, the rudder, the elevators, all of a sudden there was weight to everything, a certain resistance that felt solid, powerful, and made me feel, even though it was my first real taste, in control. Even here in the driveway my heart rate was up; even though there would be no flying today, that feeling of nervous excitement burned through me as though I stood perched at the very edge of a towering cliff ready to leap into a freefall before pulling my chute; I will never forget the sound the engine made as it coughed and sputtered to life—sort of like an old Volkswagen Beetle crossed with a tractor—after Southy called "Contact!" and threw the propeller to get it going and shouted above the din "Choke! Choke! Choke!" with which, in my nervousness, I operated too eagerly, causing us to become lost in a dense cloud of white fumes and causing Southy to shout "More power! More power! More power!" in order to clear the flooded motor, which eventually it did and I sat there, mindful of holding the brake on hard, with that substantial blade behind me whomping the air at several hundred revolutions per minute, each one feeling so close that it could have taken my head off; the sound was deafening, especially when I squeezed the throttle and brought up the revs, and I was thankful for Southy's later reminder that, once I was underway, I would leave all the noise behind me. We'd done it; we were ready with about a week up our sleeves, which was just as well because I still had to organise the various props, people to accompany us out to the old Plumpton paddock, as well as a large tent in which we would keep the aircraft and all necessary equipment for its maintenance; I also, like Houdini himself, wanted a chance to take the Voisin up before the day in question (hopefully my recce wouldn't end up like Houdini's in Hamburg, with the machine in the hedge), but ultimately this would prove impossible, for on arriving out there, greeting the man from whom we were kindly granted access to the paddock, a grain farmer by the name of Wayne Booth, we not only had to set everything up in order for it to be just so—which would take two full days—but we were met with inclement weather where intermittent patches of heavy rain were pushed along by gusty winds—in his spirited drawl Wayne informed us that we were too late, the centenary celebrations of the Houdini flight had already taken place, obviously, ten years before, in 2010, an event for which he'd also made his paddock available (we were lucky Houdini had made his flight in mid-March, for it was then that the paddock had been harvested and was awaiting the sowing of a fresh crop); but while we might have been lucky in this respect, we were not so lucky in terms of the weather, and when we showed Wayne the aircraft and explained the match test to him, he removed his full-brim hat, cast his eyes up to the heavens and told us that we might be late on that front too, the weather was becoming increasingly unpredictable, the seasons were shifting around and hard to gauge, the hot stretches were staying hotter for longer, bushfires were becoming more frequent and deadly, and it was a long time since the wind hadn't raced across these plains at least part of each day; in fact, Wayne said as he straddled the quad bike on which he'd ridden over to our tent by a small dam, if we'd come knocking a year later he wasn't sure if we'd be talking to him or someone else—"Maybe there'll be no-one out here"—for he and his wife Christine and their son Stuart were on the brink of selling up and moving to the city, the elements were too unreliable and more often than not lately unforgiving, "Sometimes you'll have a good year, but more and more you just don't know. It's too uncertain. Unpredictable. You can't live your life that way, in chaos," he said to us abandoning his bike and coming under the tent now in order to escape a sudden downpour that pulsed against the canvas, "I'll be sad to see her go," he said seemingly to the rain that was being blown into the tent as Southy told me to help him push the aircraft further inside, "and maybe we could stick it out; maybe it's just part of a larger weather cycle, but it's just too up in the air, too brutal when it fails. But," he said taking in a breath, "we haven't decided for sure yet.

Maybe things will turn around in the next year or so." I told him I was sure they would, I was sure he would find a way, but what I meant was that I hoped he'd find a way, for how could I be sure? As it happened, to my great disappointment, I wouldn't have the opportunity to take the Voisin up before 18 March; although we waited in that tent, minute by minute, hour by hour, throughout the days in the lead-up, Southy returned from wandering the field with the words, "Too much wind! Too much wind!" and we would retreat into our books, or into music, or into reading articles on the internet until an hour or two later when the whole process would be repeated and Southy would again come back muttering to himself, "Too much wind. Too much wind," and cursing the flatness of the land and its apparent unendingness; and so 18 March came and went and still the wind did not let up, not even for an hour, not even for a quarter of an hour; Southy's match barely even held a flame before it was snuffed out and the grey smoke sent horizontally on its way—"Too much wind. Too much bloody wind!"—it was a question of how long we could hold our nerve, for there was something appealing to the idea of simply throwing caution to the literal wind and having a go, but then, to be honest, if ever I had a look of impatience in my eye, Southy was alert to it and would say to me, "Don't even think about it," in a voice and with a look that told me he was more concerned for the Voisin than he was for me, that he would not have me chucking two years of his work into the sizeable trunk of one of the eucalypts that lined the field; what was worse, I had to organise for my audience to be ready at a moment's notice, which was all right to begin with—I'd managed to convince nine of my former fellow performers, including Vasily, who'd been so instrumental in the conception of the whole idea, to play along with the full recreation, including costumes and blocking and someone to play Ralf C. Banks, another to play the journalist, and another still to wield a Kodak Brownie No. 2—but as time wore on it became impractical, and when the calls started to come in and the voices on the other end were saying they couldn't make it today, I felt the dream start to slip away. Yet I kept the faith, for all we needed was one calm, still day, even just half a day; but the wind would not let up; it was like a plague, all-pervasive and unrelenting, not quite strong enough to blow our tent from its pegs but certainly strong enough to keep our wheels on the ground; and, of course, I was unable to stay overnight, I had Dad to consider, it was bad enough that I was spending my days on that blustery plain waiting for a break that was not forthcoming; I did not intend to be neglectful, I did not intend for this process to take us any further than 18 March, exactly one hundred and ten years since Harry Houdini became THE FIRST SUCCESSFUL AVIATOR IN AUSTRALIA, and although we'd missed the mark it wasn't as if we could just abandon the whole project, that would have been madness, we were both of us, and Vasily too, my stout champion, committed to getting off the ground, which meant that although we weren't recreating that record-making flight, we were recreating the rigmarole of, just as the Master himself had done, driving out to the paddock each morning at dawn, inspecting the aircraft, checking the weather against the forecast and conducting the match test before deciding there was too much wind, far too much wind, too dangerous today, and repairing to the tent to await our opportunity or simply getting back in the car and driving home again. And we're still at it, months later; some days now we fire up the machine and I practice taxiing across the bumpy terrain to get a feel for being in motion, for the weight of the controls, for the wind on my face, which often is enough to get my imagination going, soaring in fact, and looking down at my white aviation suit, my shirt and tie, the thick (almost blinding, it must be said) rims of my old aviation goggles, the smells and sounds of the motor, I am thrust back into that time of pioneers, I am standing on the precipice of the twentieth century looking down over it as though it is a sprawling plain below me, a nod towards the age into which we've been thrust, a look at the birth-place of aviation, like Zaharie's Penang, and there off in the distance, just inside the horizon, the hazy shapes of the twenty-first century are already something more than a mirage but also something less than solid, tangible matter, an illusion but also very real, a bizarre commingling of outdated things and ideas together with unfathomable advances and possibilities, and on those mornings racing up and down the old Plumpton paddock, bounding over rocks and ruts in the soil, I inch the wheel forward for lift, just a touch, just to see, to feel, maybe I will get away with it, maybe not, because I want nothing more than to head over to that far-flung place on the horizon, to rise into it, to slip the bonds of today and flash forward into the world of tomorrow, into a time when forgetting and not knowing have been relegated to the past, a time when not only is every fact, datum or titbit literally at our fingertips, but contained, captured, within our very brains, when we can survey everything around us and nothing will escape us and we are hardwired into the world, when we are in control of it all, absolutely everything; to leave the present behind, the patterns, the repetitions, and strike out into uncharted waters as pioneers into the great unknown, to discover new worlds, new ways of being, and never return.

Publisher's Note

Most of the images reproduced in this book are out of copyright and in the public domain. Others are publicly available but lack a clear attribution sufficient to determine a place of origin. Among these images are all those that can be dated to the mid-twentieth century, as well as the photograph of the memorial plaque at Diggers Rest and the diagram of the Immelmann turn. Still other images have been made available via the channels noted in the text: the photograph of the model rescue plane belonging to Zaharie Ahmad Shah originates from the Facebook page established in memory of him, while the screenshot of his flight simulator map appears in the Royal Malaysia Police Forensic Report detailing the official response to the disappearance of MH370. The only image not in the public domain or made available in the public interest is the photograph of Johnny Bègue on page 130. This image originates from Imaz Press Réunion. However, despite the publisher's best endeavours to seek permission to reproduce it, all enquiries remain unanswered and unacknowledged at the time of publication of this book. As such, the image appears here on the basis that, under the laws of the United Kingdom, the requirement to undertake best endeavours to seek permission has been satisfied to the fullest extent possible under the prevailing circumstances. Any parties with a demonstrable interest in the rights to this image may contact the publisher in writing via www.ThisIsSplice.co.uk.

SPLICE

ThisIsSplice.co.uk

Lightning Source UK Ltd.
Milton Keynes UK
UKHW010017130922
408763UK00004B/1121